# Death by Brisket

## A LAS CHICAS DE CARNE MYSTERY

### BOOK ONE

## LEAH R CUTTER

KNOTTED ROAD PRESS

**Death by Brisket**
**A Las Chicas de Carne Mystery: Book One**
Copyright © 2025 Leah Cutter
All rights reserved
Published by Knotted Road Press
www.KnottedRoadPress.com

ISBN: 978-1-64470-514-8

Cover Art:
ID 128935154 | Meat steak isolated illustration © madozi | Depositphotos.com

Cover and interior design copyright © 2025 Knotted Road Press

### Reviews
It's true. Reviews help me sell more books. If you've enjoyed this story, please consider leaving a review of it on your favorite site.

### Come someplace new...
Do you enjoy exploring strange new worlds, new cultures, new people?

Journey into the various lands envisioned by Leah R Cutter.

Sign up for my newsletter and I'll start you on your travels with a free copy of my book, *The Island Sampler.*

http://www.LeahCutter.com/newsletter/

### Buy More!
Did you know that you can buy directly from the Knotted Road Press website?

https://www.knottedroadpress.com/

# Also by Leah R Cutter

**Magazine**

*Mystery, Crime, and Mayhem*

***Urban/Contemporary Fantasy Series***

**Seattle Trolls**

*The Changeling Troll*

*The Princess Troll*

*The Fairy-Bridge Troll*

*The Troll-Demon War*

*The Troll-Human War*

*The Troll-Troll War*

**The Witch's Progress**

*Circle of Air*

*Circle of Fire*

*Circle of Water*

*Circle of Earth*

**The Chronicles of Franklin**

*Franklin Versus The Popcorn Thief*

*Franklin Versus The Soul Thief*

*Franklin Versus The Child Thief*

**The Clockwork Fairy Kingdom**

*The Clockwork Fairy Kingdom*

*The Maker, the Teacher, and the Monster*

*The Dwarven Wars*

*For all those who have earned their "stripes."*
*As well as for my husband who's had to put up with me learning the ropes.*

# One

I'd like to start this off by making the record crystal clear.

I am *not* a witch.

Have I been told that the meat rubs and sauces that I invent are magical? Absolutely.

I've even been called a wizard in the kitchen when it comes to the other *accoutrements* that I make, such as my beer-garlic bread, my grilled and stuffed mushrooms, and even my white-chocolate cranberry-orange pistachio truffles.

I have no true magic, though, at least according to my girlfriend Gabby.

And she should know, as she's *actually* a witch. A fire witch, to be precise.

She and I, along with her sister Cecilia, make up the BBQ competition team known as Las Chicas de Carne.

I know, I know. How did this Brit from London with a properly hyphenated surname (Elanor Montgomery-Hysmith) end up with two Hispanic-Americans cooking barbecue? Shout me a beer and I'll tell you sometime. Or better yet, a proper scotch.

Currently, it was the Monday after the BBQ, Beer, and Brats competition held in Little Bavaria, a town in the Cascade mountain range of Washington state. Some brilliant marketer back in the 1980s had decided that every building in the town should look as though it was part of a small German village, with peaked roofs, faux Tudor fronts, and small second-story balconies holding planter boxes filled with equally faux greenery.

The contest had been held at one of the larger parks, just east of the main tourist-trap town center. We'd done quite well, taking third in chicken, seventh in ribs, second in brisket, but twenty-second in pulled pork. (I was going to have to talk with Gabby about what had happened to the pork. Judges had declared it dry. My pork is *never* dry.)

We'd camped a few miles away outside town. Whenever we arrived at a new campground, I was never certain which side of the Yanks I'd get: the generous side or the stingy side. Or both, occasionally.

This place was more generous. Large pine trees stood guard between the allotted camping slabs. Each site had a small firepit and a rather large, if uncomfortable, picnic table. We not only had an electrical hookup for the motorhome, we could also use their water. Plus, there was a place to dump out our waste close to the entrance of the grounds.

Chill air had greeted me as I'd stepped outside the motorhome that morning, making me glad for my heavy coat, jeans, boots, and wooly cap. The bloody birds were going mad. Some of the areas we traveled to were so filled with them that I feared going deaf. The smell of smoke still lingered, possibly from our campfire the night before, or possibly from Gabby.

I found her lounging in one of the camp chairs that we'd brought with us. She didn't need any extra layers—her fire magic always kept her warm. She wore her long black hair in her usual single braid, though without flowers decorating it. Her peach-colored, long-sleeved T-shirt nicely set off her dark skin. Light makeup that morning, just a touch of a pale eyeshadow and pink lips.

After glancing at her, I knew better than to disturb her.

She had that far-away look in her eyes that I'd grown to both love and hate.

Love, because it meant that she was employing her *farsense* technique. I teased her about it sometimes, calling it the supernatural hotline.

Chances were, someone needed our help, and we would soon be off on a new adventure.

Hated it, because we *were* scheduled for another barbecue competition—The Stary Nights BBQ Festival—that coming weekend, out on the coast, in a town called Starhaven.

Sometimes we had to cancel at the last minute because Gabby's visions took us too far away. (Bowing out so late also meant we didn't get our entrance fees back, either. As I was in charge of the money for the team, that always hurt.)

Plus, we occasionally lost contests on account of Gabby being too distracted by whatever supernatural shenanigans were going on.

And I bloody hated losing.

We did the competitions for many reasons. Primarily, they worked as adverts. Gabby and Cecilia's cousins operated our food truck (also called *Las Chicas de Carne*) back at our home base of San Francisco. And who wouldn't want to go eat award-winning barbecue in their neighborhood? We were still saving up for an actual brick and mortar establishment. I estimated that it would take another couple of years for us to get there.

Possibly longer if we kept getting pulled away from contests by some sort of mystery.

That was the other reason to attend a barbecue competition: the prize money. For most contests, the top three entries in each category of meat (brisket, ribs, pulled pork, and chicken) would get a cash reward. For the larger contests, it was the top five. They also had a grand champion, that is, the team who'd earned the most points by placing high in all the categories. That, too, came with prize money.

The really big competitions had three levels of champions, with commensurate levels of compensation.

We'd been doing well with the Left Coast BBQ Association, or LCBA. I actually preferred the contests out here, as opposed to the ones managed by the KCBA, or Kansas City BBQ Association, out on the east coast. (Yes, I'm well aware that Kansas City, itself, isn't on the east coast. But the KCBA does run many of the contests all up and down the entire east side of the ridiculously large landmass called the USA.)

Not because the KCBA ran their contests in an unprofessional manner. No, it was because all the judges were trained by the KCBA to prefer sweet to savory.

Personally, I'd much rather have a properly salted and seasoned piece of meat to something that tasted like it had a sticky candy coating on it. (They call them chicken-leg lollies for a reason.)

So I sat myself down on the hard wooden bench connected to the picnic table, wrapped my hands around my still piping hot cuppa, and waited for Gabby to come back from wherever she was.

Of course, I'd created the tea blend I used that morning.

I'd started with a decaffeinated English Breakfast tea, to which I'd added bergamot oil, lemon grass, dried orange peel, dried ginger, spearmint, licorice root, cocoa nibs, and powdered vanilla.

And yes, it was as delicious as it sounds: the nibs and the tea itself made it rich and full, while the other ingredients gave it pops of brightness. The splash of heavy cream added a luscious mouth-feel. Overall, it was just divine.

As a child, I hadn't ever gone camping or even that bastardization called glamping. I firmly believe that both of my parents were allergic to dirt as well as anything that smacked of DIY. I'd had some level of culture shock the first few times I'd stayed out in the woods, but as we were in a proper motorhome and not in a tent, I grew to think of it as our personal traveling motel room. Plus, I was still young enough to enjoy the adventure—not quite thirty yet, though that was looming in the next year. Gabby was older, at thirty-three, while Cecilia was at the ripe old age of thirty-five.

When the three of us were together, strangers would peg Cecilia as the youngest and me the oldest. Mother had always said I was born with an old soul or some such rot. I prefer to think it's because I'm the responsible one in the group.

Well, most of the time.

Cecilia was the "face" of the group. She had modelesque features, stood almost five foot eleven, and exuded an enviable calm as well as charm. I was shorter, at five foot eight. Gabby stood the shortest, at merely five foot three. I may have occasionally referred to her as my pocket girlfriend, though usually when she wasn't in hearing range.

Finally, I heard Gabby sigh. I looked over my shoulder and spotted her stretching and yawning. Then she heaved herself out of the chair and came to sit beside me.

While she didn't put her arm over my shoulders—neither

of us really went for that sort of PDA—she did lean against my arm.

Her natural (supernatural?) warmth instantly penetrated my layers and I felt much cozier. I loved having my own personal fire hearth.

"So where are we off to?" I asked.

Cheeky git stole my cuppa and took a large sip before she replied.

"We're still going to Starhaven, to The Stary Nights BBQ Festival," she said, her voice rough as if she hadn't used it in a while, despite the tea. "We need to deal with what happened the next town over."

"Can you tell me about it?" I asked gently. Sometimes Gabby wanted to talk about what she'd seen. Sometimes, it was too close, too fresh, and she needed a while to chew on it.

Those far away events almost always happened in real time. Occasionally, it was something in the past. She never saw the future though, at least as far as I knew.

Her friend AJ was a water witch. Those sorts dealt with the future. Whereas air witches dealt with the past. Fire and earth were both present tense, as it were.

Gabby nodded, and leaned more heavily on me for a moment before she straightened herself up.

"Young man was killed," Gabby said. "Pushed off a bridge. The sheriff just declared it a suicide. But it wasn't. And his ghost..." Gabby paused, shivering. "This ghost is *angry*."

"I take it that isn't good?" I asked. While we'd dealt with ghosts before, I didn't recall Gabby describing any of them as angry.

Gabby nodded. She turned wide eyes to me.

"His soul is trapped in the bridge. His anger makes him

strong. He's already starting to weaken the bridge supports. It will take some time, but..."

"I see." And I did.

While the bridge wouldn't collapse tomorrow if we didn't hurry up and get there, its shelf life had been seriously compromised.

We would have to solve this mystery and free this poor soul. Gabby wouldn't agree to leave the area until she'd fixed the problem. Hopefully this Starhaven wasn't about to become our "base" for the rest of the year.

"Let's get packing, then," I told her.

There's no graceful way to stand up from a picnic table bench. I still managed as well as I could, holding out my hand to Gabby to help her up, giving it a quick squeeze before releasing it.

"Yeah, I suppose we should go sooner rather than later," Gabby said. "I'll call Cecilia."

"Good luck," I said, gulping down the last of my tea before heading inside the motorhome. I had a lot to do before we could hit the road.

Cecilia had stayed that night at a hotel in town. Possibly with company. We never begrudged her the night "off" as it were. Gabby and I had each other.

Plus, the nights Cecila was gone meant that Gabby and I could spend a bit more time with each other.

Always put a smile on my face the next morning.

So I banged about in the motorhome, strapping down pans, spices, everything that was loose in the kitchen before tackling our bedroom. Gabby joined me after a few minutes, and in no time at all we were ready to hit the road.

And off to our next adventure.

# Two

I always found it so quaint how the Yanks insisted on proclaiming their heritage. Cute towns like Starhaven were well protected, with plenty of brass plaques full of historical trivia adorning the few brick buildings remaining in the downtown area.

The National Trust would politely decline their application to be put on any sort of register. Not unless something truly important had happened here.

However, for most of its life, Starhaven had been just another port city, shipping wood and other commodities to Asia and other more civilized parts of the world.

It had taken us most of the day to drive from the mountains to the coast. Both Cecilia and I drove. While Gabby could drive, and occasionally did, it was always safer to have her as a passenger. Her *farsense* snuck up on her occasionally. It wasn't as bad as say, someone with seizures. She had some awareness of her surroundings and could get herself off to the side of the road.

However, the two vehicles we had were of the larger variety. I generally drove the motorhome with Gabby riding beside me. While Cecilia's vehicle was only a four-door pickup truck, she also hauled the rather big trailer behind her. It was loaded with Inez, our offset smoker, the UDS (ugly drum smoker), and all the rest of our equipment, including a bulky, insulated container that held all the spices and rubs we had for sale. No one wanted Gabby trying to manage all that when the supernatural hotline started ringing.

After such a long trip, the pair of them agreed that we all needed to stretch our legs for a bit. So we unhooked the trailer and Gabby drove the truck from our campsite into town. Though it wasn't far away, I honestly couldn't stand the thought of having to navigate even a short distance.

We wandered into one of the "old" buildings that held a market, poking our noses into the various shops, seeing if anything struck our fancy for dinner. I picked up a few more fresh herbs. (No, I do not have a problem, despite how Gabby rolled her eyes at me—I just don't want to run out.)

Cecilia drew the most attention, of course. She had the sort of beauty that could take your breath away if she smiled at you just right. Like me, she had no magic, though I would swear that she could, at will, turn the charisma dial up to eleven.

After one or another of us had vetoed all the "charming" restaurants in the marketplace (too commercial by half) Gabby held up her phone.

"How does authentic British fish and chips sound?" she asked coyly.

I opened my mouth then shut it again.

"It sounds marvelous, but chances are, I'll be disappointed in the end, won't I?" I said.

Gabby nodded. "That's a possibility. But this place has rave reviews. From people claiming to be English. And they're an actual local establishment."

Cecilia nodded. "Lead the way," she said.

It couldn't be too bad, could it?

Oh, who was I kidding? It was likely to be bloody awful.

I still followed dutifully along, trying not to get my hopes up.

"I must say, I do have to give them points for style," I admitted as we walked through the car park and up to the restaurant.

Though I use that term in only the loosest possible sense.

It wasn't a food truck, either.

Instead, it was a food *boat*. Some mad cracker had gotten it into their head that they should serve fish and chips out of an antique red-painted wooden boat on the edge of a car park. Hard wooden picnic tables graced the boulevard beside the area.

The air smelled amazing as we drew closer, that hot grease scent that promised the crispiest golden delights.

Three people stood in the queue before us, while another four soon gathered behind.

"Popular place," Cecilia commented.

"With Yanks," I murmured.

Gabby elbowed me in the ribs. "Play nice."

I sighed but kept my commentary to myself.

The menu was refreshingly short. That meant they specialized, and hopefully the few things that they did cook, they did well. They offered proper malt-vinegar cups to go along with the fish, the brand a familiar (and beloved) UK import.

Their hours of operation were interesting. They always

opened at a set time. However, every close time, in addition to the specific hour, had the statement, "or until we sell out."

I took it as a good sign that they sold out that frequently.

Filling the last window of the boat was a poster with a picture of a young man, announcing his celebration of life the following night.

Gabby stiffened when I pointed it out to her.

"That's him, isn't it?" I murmured softly. The supernatural hotline was really working overtime to direct us here. However, that had happened before.

Gabby nodded.

I told Cecilia about the connection, then stepped back and let her work her charms on those inside the boat.

She gave them a smile that quite frankly, if I could bottle it, I'd make three million quid. The first day.

"Hello! Welcome to *The Fish Palace*," the woman said, smiling in return. "What would you like?"

She was an older white woman, with a face that had seen so much sun and wind it was puckered and brown. Her once-brown hair had streaks of grey that didn't make her appear old as much as distinguished, the kind of look that you'd pay plenty of money to an elite hair stylist for. (Though any beautician worth their salt would have started this woman on a skin renewal regime ASAP.)

I will admit, I approved of the cheeky name for the establishment. I also approved of their choices for fish, as they offered both cod as well as haddock. I preferred the former, since I'd grown up eating that, though occasionally I'd go wild and have haddock instead.

That night, tradition held. Cecilia ordered the cod for me as well as for herself, then the haddock for Gabby, just so we could exchange bites. Along with a healthy supply of chips and extra malt vinegar. (Not that I was thinking about taking it back to the campground and using it for a sauce or something.)

"Anything to drink?" the woman prompted.

While Gabby and I appeared to be thinking about our order (of course I was having the imported UK lemonade) Cecilia was able to ask about the poster of the young man.

"Tragic," the woman said, shaking her head. "He committed suicide last week."

A voice, out of sight but from inside the boat, replied loudly, "No, he didn't!"

The woman gave Cecilia a brittle smile. "He was troubled."

"He wouldn't have ever taken his own life." A younger version of the woman moved close enough to the window for us to see.

She had the same cheekbones and broad forehead as the older woman, though her hair was a softer brown and her skin had been properly conditioned, leaving it white and supple, with just a few cute freckles sprinkled across her nose.

"We're so sorry for your loss," Cecilia said. I could practically see the charm oozing from her as she continued. "Can you tell me what happened?"

"Not now," the woman said to her daughter, holding up a finger in warning.

The girl gave a rather impressive eyeroll, but nodded.

"Any drinks?" the woman repeated, determined to move us along and get to the rest of the queue piling up behind us.

I had the lemonade, Cecilia took a flier on the blackcurrent soda, while Gabby stuck with water.

Gabby and I staked out an end of one of the picnic tables while Cecilia waited for our food. She looked triumphant when she finally approached our chosen spot.

"Joan would love to chat with us about her best friend

Timmy after she and her mom finish up for the night," Cecilia announced, placing boxes holding yumminess on the table. "She says it'll be sooner rather than later, as they're already starting to run out of the cod."

"Let me know if I need to go back and order more," I said. As I was the one who held the purse strings, it was generally up to me about how we spent our dosh.

Attending a barbecue competition at a professional level meant a lot of expenses. First off, the teams must supply their own meat. That can run as much as four hundred dollars per contest. Plus entrance fees, which the LCBA kept reasonable. (Unlike the KCBA, who charged a premium for the larger competitions.) Then there were camping fees. State sales tax. And so on.

We were currently in the black, having received cash prizes at the last two contests, more than enough to pay for the cost of meat and other fees. I didn't think we'd win this next one, though, because Gabby was going to be so distracted. (It turned out she didn't know why the pulled pork had been dry for the previous contest, swearing that Inez hadn't overheated. Possibly it had just been the cut of meat, because it certainly hadn't been my recipe.)

The fish turned out to be amazing. The golden brown crust snapped and crunched delightfully as I bit into the first piece, savoring the hints of salt and fat as they hit my tongue. Then came the amazing, flakey fish, slightly sweet as cod generally is, melting in my mouth. The next bite, I added the vinegar, just to amp up the umami flavor.

I did *not* moan. I'm too proper to do something so wanton as that, at least in public. (In private with Gabby is a whole other matter.)

I may have whimpered. A little.

Cecilia gave me a knowing smile. "It's good, isn't it?"

I nodded and had another bite, closing my eyes. In my imagination, I was back in London at that chippy shop in one of the less reputable boroughs that had tasted this good. The wrapper had been fake newsprint, but everything else about the place had been delicious.

Just as wonderful as the fish I had in my hands.

I wasn't sure how the Yanks had done it, but I was impressed with the fish.

However, the chips weren't quite as good. They'd sat for too long after they'd been fried, and the grease had sunk into the potatoes. While they were still crisp on the outside, the insides weren't as fluffy as they could be. *The Fish Palace* needed a better holding pan to make them as top-notch as their fish.

Or we just needed to come back some night while we were here and get the chips when they were fresh out of the fryer.

Of course, my dining partners insisted on putting rank American ketchup on theirs.

"How could you defile such crispy perfection?" I demanded.

That just got me snickers and an eyeroll from Cecilia and Gabby, respectively.

"And how can you put vinegar on yours?" Cecilia teased back. "They're salty enough."

"Heathen," I called her.

"You could use mayo," Gabby suggested helpfully.

"I'm English. Not a continental," I said as priggishly as possible.

That earned me more sniggers.

We dawdled over dinner, even going up and ordering

another batch of chips, this time, fresh from the fryer and gobs-mackingly delicious.

In a little less than an hour's time, the sign went up about being sold out, and they had to turn away the last few people already queued up. After they'd shuttered the windows, it wasn't too long before this Joan stepped out of the back of the boat.

"Show time," I murmured to the others. I generally took a backseat to these sorts of discussions, letting the others run them.

That turned out to be a good choice.

# Three

"Timmy didn't kill himself," Joan insisted. She'd brought yet another serving of chips to our table and was heartily munching them herself.

No one begrudged her a little comfort food, though I was surprised that she still found them so tasty after slinging them around every evening.

Then again, they were rather addictive. I may have snuck a few myself. After dipping them in one of the remaining vinegar cups, of course.

Though the afternoon had started off warm, as evening had approached it had gotten chilly. I sat beside Gabby so at least half of me was toasty. Poor Cecilia sat across the table and looked a bit cold. Joan had the appropriate layers for the Pacific Northwest, so wasn't bothered a bit.

"Why do you say that?" Cecilia asked, taking the lead as always.

Joan blew out a breath, allowing her lips to flap like a horse's. (If I'd ever made such a noise, my mother would have likely signed me up for addition classes in decorum.)

"Mom's right, in a way. Timmy was troubled. I'd known him his entire life. He'd gotten into drugs as just a kid. Never had to spend time in juvie, but that was just because the cops couldn't make any arrest stick," Joan said. "However, he'd been cleaning up his act. He'd been sober for ten months." She sighed. "I know some people didn't believe that, that he'd back-slid again recently, but I had faith in him."

"How old was Timmy?" Gabby said.

That surprised me. I figured that she would have known the exact date and time he'd been born—ghosts tended to be talkative that way, telling you all about their former lives while complaining about their current circumstances. Then again, this was an *angry* ghost. Maybe he hadn't been as chatty?

"Twenty-three," Joan said. "We're both Scorpios."

I didn't give that the eyeroll that it deserved. Then again, not many people were aware that magic, *real* magic, existed. Instead, they clung to whatever intangible wisps of the fantastic that they could spin up for themselves.

"We were both born in November, three days apart," Joan said, warming to the topic. "When we were kids, we used to celebrate our birthdays together."

"So if he didn't take his own life, what happened?" Cecilia said, drawing Joan's attention back to her and that beatific smile she wore. It radiated comfort and understanding, like that wooly jumper of your mum's that you might have stolen before heading off to Uni. (Not that I'd done something like that. On the other hand, Melba, our cook, may have been missing one or two pieces of comfort clothing.)

Joan made that horse-like noise again. I fought against how my back stiffened at the noise.

I was *not* becoming my mother, automatically disapproving of such things. Really.

"I'm not sure," Joan said softly. "He had this girl he liked."

Even though I'm not the one who's the best with people—not everyone understands or appreciates my dry English sense of humor—even I could hear the regret in that little statement.

*He had this girl he liked...who wasn't me.*

"Can you tell us about her?" Cecilia prompted.

"Her name's Leticia. She's not from around here. Her parents retired here? Or something? Anyway. They met at the *Icy-Freeze*, where he was working. She kept coming by and flirting with him," Joan said, still sounding disapproving.

"Do you suspect Leticia may have killed him?" Gabby asked, picking up the thread.

"I don't think Leticia would do something like that herself. But she was popular with a lot of guys. Like, a lot," Joan said. "She was stringing them all along, like she was Timmy. Maybe one of them got jealous or something."

That didn't really square up if Timmy was just another of her pack. That only made sense if Timmy was at least slightly more important than the others.

And if that were the case, we'd be seeing a rash of additional murders in the area. Which hopefully was not about to happen. Gabby's supernatural hotline never reported future crimes, so we wouldn't know about any of the killings until after the fact.

"Do you know of any of the others who were being strung along?" Cecilia asked.

"Why do you want to know?" Joan said, finally twigging to the fact that we were complete strangers and asking a lot of questions.

"My brother killed himself," I said, jumping in when the sisters paused for just a moment too long. I was weaving a story out of whole cloth, as I'd been an only child, a "one-and-done deal," at least according to my mother. "Your Timmy looked a bit like him. And the anniversary of Samuel's death is coming up next month."

Joan reached her hand out to me in an unwelcome gesture of sympathy. I still grasped her greasy, cold fingers for a moment before letting them go.

Unfortunately, it was impolite for me to immediately reach for the hand sanitizer that I kept in my purse. Even I wouldn't stoop so low, despite the current temptation.

"I'm sorry for your loss," Joan said. "Timmy would have been, too."

I gave her the proper nod for the comment, then sat back and let the others handle it again.

Hopefully I hadn't stuck my foot into it too much.

"How old was Samuel when he transcended?" Joan asked.

It took me a moment to translate her words into sense. "He'd just reached his majority," I told her. Then *I* had to translate. "Twenty-one. Though the trust wouldn't have kicked in until he was twenty-five. But he'd just failed Uni, and my parents were less than understanding." I personally had had brilliant marks, despite being thoroughly uninterested in the subject matter. I'd always been sneaking away to cook up delicious treats whenever I could rather than study more corporate law.

"That's rough," Joan said.

"He was actually troubled," I assured her. "No question of who ended his existence."

"But you don't think Timmy would have killed himself?" Cecilia asked, trying to get the train back on the right track.

"No," Joan said firmly. "He was starting to be happy. Smiling more."

I could tell the admission left small cuts in her heart, that someone else had been making him happy and not her.

"He was renting a room at a place he called the slop house," Joan told us. "Him and three other guys. He used to complain about the mess all the time. For the last few weeks, he'd started taking steps to make it a better place. Cleaning up after himself and getting the others to do the same." She gave us a true smile, possibly the first that evening. "Two weekends ago, he organized what he called a *summer scour*, offering free pizza to his friends, doing a deep clean of every room. I went to help. Leticia was there, though she was pretty useless. Some of our other friends went as well."

Joan paused, shaking her head. "He seemed so proud of himself, looking at how that place shone afterward. Then he went and killed himself later that night? Not a chance."

I could see her point. That didn't sound like a troubled bloke.

Cecilia gave Joan the company email and phone number, as we really didn't want to hand out our personal information to strangers. We agreed to meet again the next day. Joan would take us on a tour of the town, show us the slop house as well as the bridge.

"I'm truly sorry for your loss," Joan said to me just before she left.

I nearly asked her what she meant before I remembered dear departed Samuel.

"Just as I am for yours," I assured her. Though possibly my sentiment had more of a smattering of truth behind it.

On our walk back to the truck, we chatted about what we'd just heard, but didn't come to any conclusions.

The morning would hopefully bring us illumination. And

perhaps a resolution of this sad story, though I doubted we'd be that lucky. Even with the supernatural hotline working overtime.

# Four

Cecilia declined joining us for our meetup the next morning. She was our webmistress and saw to our social media presence. She still needed to post pictures from the latest competition, as well as update the awards page with our most recent prizes. Plus create a new video for her own personal feed, probably something to do with makeup despite how little Cecilia actually wore or needed.

It was always hit or miss if the campground we were staying at would have WiFi access. Evidently, the one we were at had screamingly fast access, at least during the middle of the week when the grounds weren't completely packed to the gills.

So it was just Gabby and I heading into town after a lovely bowl of chicken soup with rice and garlic for breakfast. I felt certain that she and I could handle the meeting with Joan, that we'd get all the information we'd need. Maybe even figure this mystery out before the weekend.

Though I had opened my big mouth and mentioned my beloved, deceased, totally fictional brother Samuel. (Thank goodness Gabby remembered what I'd named him. Otherwise, I might have started calling him Jacob or something.)

The town was partially hidden by the looming pine forests as we drove in, so we didn't get a good view of it until we were almost on top of it. The ocean lay in the far distance, a gray line across a gradually brightening sky. The welcome sign had been commemorated by some official bloke sixty years before, so of course, it was as venerated as the "old" downtown.

I had my tea in a to-go mug (one of ours, natch, branded with the Las Chicas logo, showing two Hispanic women in *Dia de Muertos* makeup holding BBQ implements), while Gabby insisted on finding coffee on our way to meet Joan.

While I occasionally went over to the dark side and had a cup, I didn't trust even the chain establishments to actually give me decaf. I'd had more than one occasional mixup, making the risk not worth it. (Me on caffeine is not a pretty sight. More like a drunkard with serious DTs.)

Most mornings, Gabby would make her own "nectar of life" as she called it. However, she did like exploring and finding new coffee beans.

She was just fortunate that I had a use for those extra beans, either as chocolate-covered treats or making a batch and using the coffee in one of my sauces. I had a marvelous rub that combined instant espresso coffee, dark cocoa powder, and black pepper. In a pinch, I would let her use my instant, though she insisted that on its own, it tasted foul.

The little shop we found appeared to be something of a community gathering place, as it advertised "sip and paint" classes, a regular book club, and even a "Mom's night off" event. The barista was properly surly, as I'd been informed that the quality of the beans goes down if the staff is happy. That did make it difficult to chat her up, and there was no handy poster about Timmy's upcoming celebration of life.

Gabby tried unsuccessfully to charm the barista. But as much as I love my little fire witch, none of us mere mortals had the charisma that Cecilia did.

So we walked out not empty handed as Gabby clutched her coffee to her chest, but with no further clues about what was going on.

All that was left was to head to our meeting with Joan.

She met us at a car park that was a block away from the "slop house." She was already there, waiting in her car, sipping her own drink.

"Oh!" she exclaimed when we drew up next to her. "I'm so glad you came!"

Gabby suffered a hug from the girl, as did I. I never understood why the damned Yanks were so touchy-feely. Just because we'd expressed some interest in her unrequited love's death didn't mean we were bosom buddies.

Yanks are weird.

"I wanted you to get a feel for the entire neighborhood," Joan explained when I asked if one of the houses directly across the street was our intended snooping spot.

Did she really? Or was she afraid of being labeled a stalker? Inquiring minds and all that.

So we headed off down the street. The neighborhood was only slightly dodgy. While a few of the houses had car parts as lawn ornaments, and others had weeds threatening to overtake the buildings, most of them looked clean and well taken care of.

The slop house was no exception. Yes, the lawn had only recently been trimmed—what little grass remained was in shock and browning rapidly due to its unexpected exposure to sunlight. And the house certainly needed a new coat of paint. But the roof didn't have a faded blue tarp on it, unlike its neighbor's, who was obviously trying to prolong needing to go up there and actually fix a hole. The couches sitting under the front eves looked comfy enough, though I would lay money down that they stank of mold. And the glass in the windows appeared hearty and whole.

Joan lingered a moment. Gabby did as well.

It totally did *not* make me uncomfortable. Really. Three young women just standing on the pathway and gawking at the house of a recently deceased individual.

I would allow it, though. Never knew when the supernatural hotline would ring in a clue.

Gabby's next words proved my hunch.

"Does the house seem angry to you?" she asked, her voice sounding a little wispy and far away.

"It does!" Joan said. "Though I figured that's because of Darren."

"Who's Darren?" I followed up with, since Gabby still had that far-off look in her eyes.

"One of the roommates," Joan answered. "He's always angry. When they were doing the summer scour, he and Timmy got into a huge argument. Someone went into his room without permission. It had been clearly stated that everyone's personal room was off limits," she added with a guilty shrug.

"What, did you go in there?" I asked, possibly a bit too sharply as Gabby threw me a worried look.

Joan gave me a tight smile. "No, it was Leticia. And Timmy was the one who found her there and had to remind her of the rules. But Darren walked in on them and he and Timmy got into a huge shouting match."

"What were they arguing over?" Gabby said, finally rejoining the party, as it were.

"Mainly just invasion of privacy," Joan said. "That his room was off limits for a reason."

"And that being?" I prompted.

Joan shrugged. "I don't know. Darren's always been a little off, you know?"

I struggled but I managed to contain my eyeroll at that.

No, we did *not* know, having never met any of these individuals.

"You'll get a chance to see for yourself later this afternoon. If you're coming to the celebration of life," Joan said. Then she looked at me. "Unless you think that might be too painful for you. Given your situation."

I honestly had no idea what she was on about until I remembered Samuel.

"Thank you," I said. "We'll be there, yes?" I asked, throwing a look at Gabby.

She nodded, fully back to herself.

The three of us walked around the block, looking at similar houses to what had been on the other side. I idly wondered if the one with all the bird baths was going for some sort of art installation look, or if they were just really into birds. But there was no one to ask.

Back at the car park, Joan proposed that she ride in the truck with us to the bridge.

I got the impression it wasn't so much for our sake as for hers. Needing support while going to visit the last location of her dearly departed, etc.

When Gabby gave me a look, I reluctantly nodded.

In for a penny, in for a pound.

# Five

"So how old were you when Samuel transcended?" Joan asked as soon as we were buckled up and headed down the road.

Fortunately, I'd already prepared my answers. "I was eighteen. Had just finished my A-levels."

I'd hoped that would get her sidetracked and I'd have to explain what that meant. Unfortunately, she'd seen enough British TV and understood it meant the Yank equivalent of finishing high school. (I personally blame the BBC for removing a lot of the mystique of being English, by the way.) I didn't even get the chance to go off on my rant about how *my* A-levels had had rather stringent standards compared to the lackadaisical approach they are taking these days.

"That must have been so hard!" she said, still obviously digging for more information.

"Yes, well, we soldiered on," I told her. "Left or right?" I asked before she could pummel me with more questions or questionable sympathy.

She rattled off the directions as we moved forward again.

"Did you know right away that he'd killed himself?" Joan asked.

I really don't understand why Yanks believe that it is their god-given right to pry as they do.

"Finding him hanging on the end of a rope with his suicide note conveniently pinned to the body was good enough for us," I said dryly.

"And there couldn't have been anyone else who'd done it?" Joan pressed.

"What, the butler?" I snarked. "No. Samuel was, as you said, troubled. He'd made a previous attempt before, stealing a bottle of Mother's sleeping pills. And he'd made an effort to say goodbye. At least that was what I think he was doing, in retrospect."

I wasn't about to bloody go into what that had been. Let her work it out for herself.

"See, Timmy would have done that if he'd been about to kill himself," Joan said, taking up the thread. "He wouldn't have just disappeared on me. He would have wanted to say goodbye."

"And you're certain he didn't?" I asked, finally able to do a bit of my own prying.

"Yes," Joan said. "The last thing we talked about was going out to dinner the next week. He wouldn't be making plans like that if he were also preparing to jump off a bridge, right?"

I shrugged my shoulders. Who knew what a crazy Yank would do?

Then again, Gabby had already confirmed that his death wasn't a suicide, so I was prepared to be sympathetic.

"Right," I said after a bit.

"No, left, here," Joan said, continuing with her directions.

Gabby came to my rescue at that point. We'd told Joan the

previous evening why we were in town. "Would you like tickets to The Stary Nights BBQ Festival this weekend?"

Joan considered for a moment. "Yes, please. Two if you can swing it. One for me and one for my mom. She needs a break. We all do, you know?"

"Is summer your high season?" I asked. As San Francisco was such a destination city, the food truck tended to be busy all year round.

"It is!" Joan said. "*The Fish Palace* does really well during these months. We've thought about opening up for a lunch rush, but we'd have to charge less. People always are willing to pay more for dinner, you know?"

I nodded instead of reacting to that thoughtless tag that Joan continued to add to her sentences.

"Plus, we need to have enough fish for dinner. We can only store so much in the freezers on the boat." She gasped and held her hands over her mouth.

"What? What is it?" I said, glancing around. Was there a rockslide about to come crashing down on us?

"Please don't tell Mom that I mentioned we sometimes use frozen fish. Most of the people around here still believe that it's all freshly caught," Joan said.

I snorted. "Your secret is safe with us."

Then I glanced over at her. She needed a distraction. "Tell me about the recipe you use for such delicious fish. How do you make the batter? What kind of flour do you use? And do you use sparkling water?"

That finally got her off the scent of my supposed grief, as well as her real one, and talking about something that it turned out we both loved: cooking and food.

We had to leave the truck in a car park about half a mile from the bridge in order to approach it by foot. We'd ended up traveling down the coast a few miles to the next small town— Shelby—then heading inland. While there'd been a few rolling hills next to the highway we'd traveled along initially, in this area the hills were much steeper and rockier.

The trail leading from the car park to the bridge took us behind piles of bare rock that looked as though a giant had been playing at balancing stones, one upon the other. A few brave pines stuck out from the crevices, holding on for dear life. The air was warmer this far away from the constant ocean winds, and carried the scent of hard-packed dirt. Initially, the bloody birds weren't screaming at us. Then we came across a couple of very opinionated jays, unhappy with our trespassing.

Though we couldn't see the road, we could hear it, cars whizzing by without a care in the world. A couple that passed were blasting music loud enough to sound like an elongated police siren. However, as we walked, the pitch of the whooshing noise changed. I realized it wasn't cars I was listening to, but water.

We took an abrupt right around a solid wall of rock and were suddenly there, at the start of the path across the bridge. The noise level increased dramatically and the air took on a definite chill.

A raging river tumbled far underneath us, the water green with occasional whitecaps. Directly below, a hodgepodge of rocks filled the area, while further upriver, brave trees clung to the sides.

The bridge itself struck me as wide open. No struts arched over the bridge deck. All the support came from cement pillars underneath, the rounded arches gracefully carrying their load.

In addition, the area felt lonely. Don't ask me why.

Normally, bridges are connections between places. This one hung alone, aloof, a narrow, dangerous spot along the road to somewhere better.

There was only a single walking path across our side of the bridge. Anyone walking on the other side was likely to get struck by oversized mirrors, even if the driver was paying attention. A short safety wall ran along the outside edge of the walkway. Given its lack of height, it wouldn't take much of a shove for someone to topple over it.

A tunnel on the far side of the bridge swallowed (and occasionally spit out) the passing cars. The hole had been carved out of sheer rock, a vertical cliff bare of greenery. Dim lights on the tunnel's ceiling briefly highlighted each car as it passed. The smell of petrol lingered. Hopefully after the dark hole the travelers would be someplace more pleasant.

No guardrails had been placed between the cars and us pedestrians. Any fool, particularly a drunken fool, could easily get at someone they didn't like.

Cecilia had teased me more than once with the saying, "If you don't like the way I drive, stay off the sidewalk."

Was that what had happened? Had someone used their car to force poor Timmy off the pathway? Or had they accompanied him here with the promise of something?

Gabby had turned pale, though her look told me that she was mostly in the present and not gossiping on the supernatural hotline. Yet. However, she stood rock still, frozen like some damned statue.

In addition, Joan had gone fish-eyed and was possibly starting to hyperventilate.

As I appeared to be the only functioning adult in the group, I pulled up my big-girl rompers and went to talk to Joan.

"Are you okay?" I asked. Well, shouted. It was really loud there. The sound of the rushing water dominated the area.

She started, her eyes darting to me, before she gulped and nodded. "I didn't think it would be this hard," she said.

Or I think that was what she said. It was awfully difficult to hear anyone speaking in a normal tone of voice.

"Do you want to go on?" I said, glancing from one frozen person to the other. "Or just stay here for a while?"

"I need—I need to step onto the bridge," Joan said.

Gabby slowly nodded in agreement.

"All right then. Forward we go," I said.

No one moved.

"Right. You lot, follow me."

I turned and went down the few stairs (with no rail of course) to the actual bridge. A car arrived at the same time I did. The concrete under my feet bounced slightly with its passing.

Well, that was unsettling. Was the bridge always this wobbly? Or was this because of Timmy?

When I turned, I was a little surprised to find that both Joan and Gabby were directly behind me, and were also now standing on the bridge.

I glanced around, looking for one of those handy placards that would extoll the view or some "historic" fact about where we were, but there weren't any. Instead, it was just us, this bridge, and the river below.

Not knowing what else to do, I started walking again, not pausing until I reached what I judged to be the midpoint.

The view was pretty enough, I suppose, in that rough and tumble way of untamed nature. Steep walls made up the gorge, the river continuing to race away into the far distance. On the far side of the bridge, the pedestrian path continued. People probably followed the trail to somewhere nicer. Or so one hoped.

I paused, putting my hands on the cold stone of the safety wall and looked straight down. There wasn't anything to stop someone from jumping, no nets or platform below.

I was going to have to do some research. Had there been many suicides here, death by bridge, as it were? Also, how had Timmy gotten out here? Had he driven to the car park, walked up here, then offed himself? That seemed like an awful lot of planning for someone who was also scheduling dinners out.

The water below looked cold and uninviting to me. Not how I would choose to go.

I shivered and leaned back, looking to my right, past the bridge and to the embankment on the far side.

And that was when it happened.

# Six

I am *not* the one prone to visions. That is strictly Gabby's territory.

However, while I could still see the current day, the bleached concrete, the passing cars, an overlay appeared.

In the extra layer, the bridge had yet to be completed. A stark empty span gapped between the start of the deck on the far side and the finished section coming from behind me. Men in dirty clothes worked to tie the two ends together, pouring bags of something into what looked like a hand-cranked cement mixer.

A middle-aged white man, with eyes so blue they appeared extra bright compared to the washed-out appearance of his surroundings, began walking toward me. He rolled up papers as he moved, my guess was blueprints. His formerly white shirt bore sweat stains and his dark woolen trousers shed dust with every step. Old-fashioned boots covered his feet and held blobs of dripped concrete.

He grew more distinct as he came closer. The kerchief he wore tied around his neck took on a slightly red hue with a white pattern dyed into the fabric. Yellowed buttons adorned the tops of his trousers, probably to attach suspenders to.

His face gained lines and the rough whiskers of his beard stood out, a pattern of white and brown across his flat cheeks. A hawklike nose stood up proudly from the rest of his face, giving him an arrogant look. His jawline was hard and chiseled, making me think that he was used to getting his way.

*So there you are,* he said as he came to stand beside me. Or whispered. Or somehow formed words in my mind, though his lips didn't move.

He had an English accent, not posh, but not working class either. Somewhere in between. I couldn't quite place what county he was from.

"And?" I said. Or tried to say. I found my body quite frozen.

That was when I realized that the present had stopped moving. Only the overlay was active.

*Took you long enough,* he huffed at me.

"Elanor?"

The voice sounded as if it were speaking underwater. I still couldn't move or acknowledge it.

The man in front of me smirked. *See you later,* he promised.

Or threatened. Or both.

I finally could shake my head, blink my eyes.

The overlay vanished, as did the man, like the best Hollywood special effects. There one second, gone the next.

"Elanor?" Gabby asked again.

I looked over at her. I wasn't certain what my expression was, though I believe I alarmed her, as she immediately reached for my hand, peeling it off the stone railing and encasing it in her rather warm ones.

"I'm here," I said. I gulped. "I think."

"I'm sorry," Joan said. "I didn't think this would be hard for you too."

At least I didn't ask her what she was going on about.

My dear lost brother. Samuel.

Was it just my imagination working overtime? Or did I suddenly hear that ghostly man chuckling in my head, saying something like, *Yes. Samuel.*

I didn't like it. I didn't like it one bit.

Fortunately, the others agreed that we'd seen enough and leaving this place would be good for all of us.

The drive back to Starhaven was thankfully not merely uneventful but silent, as we were all wrapped up in our own thoughts.

After assuring Joan that we would be attending the celebration of life for Timmy later on that evening, we were finally shut of her and on our own.

Gabby offered to drive us back to the campground. I was shaken enough to let her.

Only after we were back, safely ensconced in the motorhome (and each other's arms), did she ask, "What happened?"

"I have no bloody clue."

I ended up repeating the encounter not just to Gabby, but then to Cecilia as well. She might have been gobsmackingly beautiful, but there was a brain behind that face. And she knew her way about the internet, more so than either Gabby or I.

"I'll do some research on the bridge," Cecilia promised us. "Do you think one of your relatives could have worked on it?"

"No idea," I said. I was just as confused as everyone else. "But be sure to look up the name Samuel."

"I will," she promised.

The sisters exchanged a look. I didn't need any magic to know that they were both worried about me.

"What?" I said, possibly a bit stroppy. "I'm fine. And besides, according to our resident expert, ghosts haunt places, not people. Right?"

Gabby nodded. "Right. So as long as you stay away from that bridge, this Samuel shouldn't bother you again."

I gave a sharp nod to that. Hopefully, I'd never have to pass by that forsaken piece of territory again.

Gabby hadn't learned anything new while standing on the bridge. Timmy was there, his soul having wormed his way between the stones. The struts holding the bridge had weakened as a result. She also felt it was a lonely stretch of the road. She hadn't been aware of Samuel at all. She had had the impression that the bridge was haunted, though she'd assumed at the time that was merely Timmy.

Did we need to do something about Samuel? Appease not merely Timmy's ghost, but Samuel's as well?

That hadn't been the impression that I'd received from the latter. Instead, it felt as though he'd been waiting for me.

Not that that had ominous overtones or anything.

To get the encounter out of my mind, I threw myself into cooking for a bit. The motorhome had an adequate setup, though I longed to upgrade the entire kitchen if we had the dosh.

We had an electric oven and a gas cooktop, supposedly the best of both worlds. In reality, I always made certain that any unnecessary electronics were unplugged before I used the oven so that we didn't blow out any fuses. Gabby regularly checked the propane lines, ensuring that nothing had shaken loose. (She'd trained herself to follow possible fire conduits with her magic, an exceedingly useful skill that we'd unfortunately had to utilize more than once.)

That afternoon, I was cooking up new sauce. I was the tender-mouth of the group. Gabby and Cecilia had suckled jalapeño juice with their mother's milk. However, that left me at an advantage, as I could accurately judge the heat levels our customers were likely to find pleasing.

I swear if left to their own devices those two would never have won a competition, and instead, would have blown out the judges' palates on the first bite.

Today was a spicy day, though. While I had a series of nightshade-free sauces that I could offer, this wasn't about to be one of them. The base began with a local fruit—marion-berries. They were similar to blackberries, but ranged both higher and lower in their taste profile, being more earthy as well as sweeter at the same time. I added a touch of cinnamon and clove to bring out more of the earthiness, followed by some powdered *lapsang souchong*, a smoked black tea.

Now, it was time to address the top notes. Molasses to augment the smoke while toning down the sweet slightly. A touch of vinegar to give it tang. Red chili flakes and smoked paprika to ramp up the volume of all the other parts. Some salt and lemon juice to brighten it up.

I kept stirring and tasting while contemplating my merely adequate spice rack. (Gabby teased me about it frequently. Certainly, I'd be the first to admit that I was small chested. However, I was not compensating for anything given the size of my spice rack. The one that I carted around with us in the motorhome barely filled my needs.)

I knew that the sauce needed something, an extra kick. Low or high notes, though? I couldn't decide.

Fate decided for me.

While reaching for the ginger—a flavor that would enhance both—I accidentally knocked the chili flakes over. A large dollop of them landed in the pot.

I dug out as much as I could, figuring that the sauce was now ruined. Only the sisters would be able to tolerate it.

Still, after I'd added some brown sugar, as well as the ginger I'd originally intended, I tried it.

The heat was on the high side of my tolerance. It was still amazing. Those chili flakes had been exactly what had been missing.

*You're welcome.*

I froze for so long I nearly scalded the sauce still simmering away on the cooktop.

That couldn't have been Samuel's voice. Ghosts only haunt places. Not people. It all had to be my imagination.

Right?

# Seven

The celebration of life was held at what could best be described as a hippy church. Oh, I didn't mind all the rainbow-colored banners on the outside, proclaiming that all were welcome there. That was actually reassuring given my avowed lesbian lifestyle.

No, it was the building itself that gave me pause.

It didn't have walls. Or a roof. Instead, it took the whole "open concept" idea to an entirely new plateau. Steel beams stuck out of the ground at regular intervals with nothing between them. The roof beams were exposed as well. Framed "windows" occurred at regular intervals, though nothing filled them.

What did they do when it rained? This was the Pacific Northwest. The annual rainfall in the area was enough to make a Scot giddy. Or did they supply rainbow-colored umbrellas for all?

We gathered in awkward clumps in the open space, under the "roof." It was probably thirty feet long and about twenty wide. Of course, there was no place to sit. Banners had been hung at the front of the church with quotes, such as: *A life that touches others goes on forever* and *Though we held you in our arms for only a little while, we will hold you in our hearts forever* and others.

I vowed to make sure to tell Gabby that my after-death party needed to be held in a pub with people getting properly leathered. Not that I was one to get legless regularly. I'd done a bit of that when I was first at Uni, and had discovered that the morning afters weren't worth it. Gabby and Cecilia both shared a love of good tequila (not that they were snobs about it, really) and had taught me how to whip up a proper margarita. In addition, a nice sipping scotch came in handy as part of a celebration after a big win, but that was about all that I or the sisters ever indulged in.

Still, I much would have preferred that to the sticky sentimentality that clung to the gathering, like an over-reduced sauce with too much sugar in it.

Joan stood toward the front of the space, her mother at her side. She waved at us when she saw us, so we joined the informal line of grievers, coming up to give her our condolences.

I suffered a hug from her. While I was close, she whispered, "Darren is to your right. Red and white striped shirt."

I didn't look right away, but instead, pulled back, squeezed her hands, and muttered something about being sorry about her loss before finally being able to escape her grasp.

After we finished expressing our sympathy, the three of us veered off to the right and reformed our own clump again. Gabby and I had a good view of Darren and his cohorts, while Cecilia faced us, giving us an excuse to be looking in that direction.

Darren was a pasty white boy with an unfortunately small

chin and beady eyes. His light brown hair could best be described as mousy. He had definitely passed from merely chunky to actively pudgy a few stones ago. And that red-and-white striped shirt wasn't doing him any favors, the broad stripes stretching across his belly making it seem extra wide.

"Victor and Robert are the other two," Gabby informed us quietly.

Cecilia nodded. "Victor's the tall one."

Huh. I was impressed that Joan managed to get all that information to the three of us.

Victor looked like the nerd of the group. Tall and thin and white, with dark brown hair, black spectacles, and a neck like a stork with a prominent Adam's apple. Both his T and his jeans were proper mourner's black. Of the three of them, he appeared to be the saddest. Recent tear tracks still marked his cheeks.

The other, Robert, wore a light blue polo and khaki slacks, the kind golf instructors have. He'd fit in well with the "sporty" set, his white face tan, though his teeth had that unfortunate florescence that came from too many treatments. He seemed extremely uncomfortable standing there, probably because there was no handy tele nearby with a footie match on.

A woman approached the group. We were close enough that I caught her name—the infamous Leticia.

Surprisingly, she wasn't a white girl but appeared Hispanic, with dark skin and black hair. She wasn't as beautiful as Cecilia (who was?) but she was pretty enough. She'd woven her black hair into a crown piled atop of her head, and like Gabby, she had tiny white flowers tucked into it, like little bells. She had on a black blouse that fit tightly across her ample chest and torso with sheer long sleeves and a short black skirt. Kitten pumps probably were the best choice for this uneven ground, but I would bet that she'd look stunning in something taller.

"Getting any sort of vibe from them?" I asked Gabby. The supernatural hotline had been ringing a lot earlier.

She slowly nodded. "Darren's angry right now. It's the same sort of emotion that came from the slop house."

"Does that mean anything?" Cecilia had to ask.

While I tried to be the most rational of the three of us, I would be lying if I didn't admit that Cecilia frequently filled that role as well.

"I don't know," Gabby said. "Maybe he believes that Timmy killed himself and is angry about that. Maybe he thinks this is all a waste of time. And someone over there has a ton of guilt as well."

"Who?" I asked.

Gabby shook her head. "If I had to peg anyone as a guilty party, I'd say it was Leticia. She's holding herself wrong."

"What would lure a young man trying to clean up his act to go up to that bridge?" I said. "Because he wouldn't just go out walkabout on his own to a place like that."

"There had to be someone else there," Cecilia agreed.

"What would they have to promise him? To get him up there?" Gabby mused.

"I wouldn't have called it a romantic getaway, that's for certain. More likely a place for a breakup," I said.

"Or a drug exchange," Cecilia added.

"How clean was Timmy? Really?" I asked quietly. "Had he cleaned up his act? Or had he backslid? And what was his relationship status with Leticia at the end?"

None of us had the answers, though I was starting to suspect that Timmy had been troubled right up until the time of his death.

We didn't get any new information at the service. A few people said some nice things, and we heard stories about how Timmy had made them laugh.

Tellingly, of the slop house boys, only Victor stood up and had a story about Timmy helping him out when his car wouldn't start one day. The other two roommates were silent. And tearless.

Laticia tried to talk about how kind Timmy had been to her, but was quickly overwhelmed with emotion. I wasn't the only one who wanted to roll my eyes, based on both Gabby's and Cecilia's expressions. What little of the story we did hear was all about her.

Now, I'm not claiming that the girl was a narcissist. However, I wouldn't have been surprised if someone came up with that diagnosis.

Had she been the one to do it? Or had she just lured Timmy to the bridge, then let someone else do her dirty work?

Neither of Timmy's parents were there. Not sure what exactly that said about the inter-family dynamics. Were they too broken up to attend? Or merely uninterested?

Timmy wouldn't have grown into a troubled lad if things had been completely hunky-dory at home.

After the ceremony, we went back to the campground to regroup. Cecilia continued her research into the history of the bridge and the making of it. She'd given me a little information —seemed a bloke named Samuel Montgomery had been one of the architects. The funding for the bridge construction had been part of the New Deal, along with the tunnel, so a little less than a century ago.

I cooked us up an amazing stew from the meat trimmings

and some fresh veggies, something that could easily be heated up for breakfast as well.

Gabby worked on her magic after that. She sat in one of the chairs next to our campfire and tried her *farsense*, to see if there was anything new on the horizon. But the supernatural hotline appeared down for the evening.

We all turned in early that night. We'd worked hard over the weekend at the previous competition, then driven for a day, and subsequently been dropped into the middle of a mystery.

Besides, the next day was going to be trying, for at least one of us.

# Eight

It wasn't just because of the date that I proposed a lay-about to Gabby the next morning, for the pair of us to sleep in and relax for the day.

However, Gabby, her hair looking adorably mussed, merely raised an eyebrow at me.

"It's the tenth," she said, as if that was all the explanation I needed.

Truth be told, it was.

With a huge put-upon sigh, I dragged myself from the warm bed, bundled up in layers of silk long-johns, sweat pants, heavy socks, two shirts, a sweater, and my woolly cap, before venturing out into the frigid early-morning air.

People don't appreciate that being in a wooded, shaded area, with nothing but trees surrounding you, is likely to drop the temp by a few degrees. It wasn't quite cold enough that I could see my breath, but it was close.

I didn't have time that morning for a proper cuppa before my call, so I decided to go for a hike while chatting.

Maybe I'd be lucky and the reception would be so horrific I wouldn't have to say much.

Dutifully, eight AM rolled around, and I picked up after the first ring.

"Hello, Mother," I said.

"Elanor, darling! How are you?" Mother's cheerful voice sounded clear over the line, despite the distance between us.

I may have been the black sheep of the entire family, but I didn't go out of my way to cause my mother pain. So we'd arranged for a phone call on the morning of the tenth of the month. No matter what was going on, I would always spend a few minutes with her. It eased things between us tremendously.

As I said, I didn't want to be an arse, no matter how much we disagreed on most everything.

"I'm good," I told my mother, being truthful. I'd slept well the previous night and wasn't quite so worn out that morning. "We did well in the last competition."

"I saw! Cecilia posted some marvelous pictures on your site," Mother commented.

Mom wasn't a complete troglodyte when it came to the internet, but she wasn't a digital native, either. About a year ago, someone had walked her through how to visit the Las Chicas de Carne website, and she'd stalked it ever since.

"It was a good cook," I said.

"What happened with the pork shoulder, though? Twenty-second? Dear, that's not like you," Mom chided.

As much as I may have cared for my mother, and I did, she was also the one who, if you managed nines across the board for your grades, with a single seven, all she'd hark on about would be the seven.

"I'm not sure," I told her. "Thank you for the reminder,

though. Gabby claims that the smoker didn't overheat, but I'm not sure."

"And how is Gabby?" Mother asked. That was more than just being polite. Though they'd never met in person, they had done some video conferencing together, even without me present.

Mother, as well as Father, had taken the whole me coming out as a lesbian thing rather well. I think they'd suspected my orientation for some time.

No, what had really stuck in Mother's craw was my choice of profession. I'd finished my third year at the University of London City, and my parents had agreed to a "skip" year before I began my apprenticeship at their hand-picked law firm.

However, that "skip" year had to look good on my CV, so after a lot of negotiations, I'd managed to get them to agree that I could take classes in international corporate law at the University of Berkeley.

The workload was pretty light, just a couple classes per semester, particularly compared to what I'd gone through the three years prior.

On a lark, I'd gone to a BBQ competition with some mates. Met Gabby and Cecilia.

The rest, as they say, was history.

"Gabby is lovely as always," I said. I never hid how much I cared for her from my parents. "And sends her love."

After a pause I asked, "And how are you and Father?"

That was my mother's cue to go into a rant about how horrible their lives were, how awful the economy was, how much it was hurting their savings.

You know. The things that mattered the most to them.

Instead, Mother said, "Oh, you know. We're making do."

"Really?" I said, surprised. "What have you been up to?"

Mother talked about her roses and her marketing club (because I truly needed to care about their investment group), as well as going round to visit Grandma Montgomery two weeks before. (Her mother was still alive and kicking, as well as preparing for the end of the world given the general collapse of all decorum among the young people. My father's parents had had the decency to pass away a few years ago, before I'd left the island.)

I told her about the coast, the camping area, and preparing for our next cook as I'd be doing a couple of practice cooks that afternoon.

All in all, the conversation was just too easy and smooth, so I was at least prepared when Mother dropped the conversational bomb, as it were.

"Well, since I know that you can't visit us during the summer due to all your competitions, we were thinking about flying across the pond to come see you," she said.

I had to stop and rewind that in my head once before I could continue.

"That might be nice," I said cautiously. I didn't want to admit how shook I was. "Is everything all right? You haven't gotten some grim health announcement that you don't want share over the phone?"

"No, deary, nothing like that," Mother said. I could hear the amusement in her voice. "It's just been such a long time since we've seen you. Five years, now! I believe that it's time for a nice long visit."

I really didn't know what my mother was playing at. Despite the fact that I was her only child, Mother had never made much of an effort to know *me*, as opposed to her version of me. I doubted she was about to correct the error of her ways. There had to be an ulterior motive.

"All right," I said cautiously. "I can email you our current itinerary for the summer, the contests that we think we're going to."

Mother had no idea that Gabby was a fire witch, and I wasn't about to educate her on that either.

Lesbian? Yes. Champion BBQ queen? All right. Consorting with witches? That might be one straw too many across the proverbial camel's back.

"That would be lovely, dear," she said.

"So, we're currently in this town called Starhaven," I said. "And the nearby town, Shelby, has a bridge that was supposedly built by some bloke named Samuel Montgomery," I said. "Know about any branch of the family who may have defected earlier? Say, in the 1930s?"

"I don't, actually," Mother said. "Why don't you ring up Grandmother Montgomery and ask her?"

I really, *really* wasn't looking forward to the lecture I was sure to get from my grandmother. However, I also could adult with the best of them, so I told Mother that I supposed I could do that.

We hung up after an hour, the conversation being a lot more civilized than usual. All right, that wasn't quite fair. Mother was almost always civil. She just didn't care for much beyond her personal sphere of influence.

What had changed? And how much was finding out about it going to suck?

That afternoon, I had a rack of ribs going in the UDS. I used natural charcoal in there, not the nasty, artificial briquets that American backyard grillers preferred. The ribs rested on the top grill of the drum while a pan of water filled with herbs and lemon slices sat at the bottom, just above the glowing coals.

Though we'd taken seventh in ribs the weekend before, I was constantly pushing at the recipe, trying to get us to number one, or at the very least in the top three, where the money was.

I knew some people who used the three-two-one method for ribs: three hours uncovered on the grill, two hours steamed, and then one last hour on the grill, with a glaze. If I didn't care about the judges, I might go that route. It produces an incredibly tender rib where the meat literally falls off the bones.

However, that wasn't what the judges were looking for. They wanted a very particular bite that was tender, flavorful, but with the meat still adhering to its support structure. So I did a modified three-two-one: generally I stuck with the first three hours, but I was experimenting with shortening the duration of the other two, say, one hour steamed and only fifteen minutes to set the glaze.

Despite the water in the drum and the general moistness of the air, I still spritzed the meat with a very tasty sauce every fifteen minutes through the first three hours of cooking.

I'd come up with a new sauce that day, one more lemon and herb based, trying to liven up the flavor just a bit. This particular spritz had gin, maple syrup, ginger and lemon juice, soy sauce, as well as some of the *lapsang souchong* brewed up into a strong tea for the smoky flavor.

I wasn't practicing my cook outside because I was afraid to go back into my kitchen. That voice I'd thought I'd heard couldn't possibly have belonged to Samuel.

Still, I wasn't giving that bastard the opportunity to haunt me there.

If it had even been him, and not my imagination. I believed Gabby when she told me that ghosts haunted places, not people. Every ghost she'd met—and there had been over a dozen at this point—had been stuck in a particular location. She'd only once heard of a ghost haunting a person, and that was a special circumstance, as both the person and the ghost were witches with powerful magic. And even then, the ghost communicated through the person's cellular. It didn't haunt the person's body.

So we all agreed that I'd probably gone slightly around the bend on that one.

Didn't mean I was going to be working inside for the next day or so. Just in case.

The ribs smelled amazing every time I lifted the cover off the drum. I was hoping that I'd managed to find a winning combination there.

While I was cooking and farting around on my phone, Cecilia came out, Gabby trailing behind her.

Given their serious expressions, I was wondering who'd stepped in it this time. Couldn't have been me, could it?

They both collapsed onto the chairs we'd brought, looking as grim as any reaper.

"What's happened?" I said, glancing at my timer. Seven more minutes before I had to get up and spritz the ribs again.

"Henry Cargill, one of the head judges for The Stary Nights BBQ Festival, was found dead this morning. He'd died sometime the previous day, in his backyard," Cecilia said. "Police are still investigating the cause of death."

I blinked, surprised. I hadn't been expecting that news at all. "Are they canceling the contest?"

"We don't know yet," Cecilia said. "I don't think they would. Too much advertising, too much money coming into the town. They can always find a new judge."

I nodded. The number of judges for a competition always depended on the number of competitors for a particular turn-in.

Say you had fifty teams competing. That meant fifty boxes of meat turned in at a specified time. According to the LCBA rules, that meant fifty judges, one for each team.

However, maybe you had a couple of teams who turned up to compete at the last minute. That would mean more judges.

Or, perhaps someone missed their turn in. You only have a ten-minute window in which to get your boxes in.

Which would mean that the contest might only have forty-nine boxes, which meant forty-nine judges. Or maybe a team looked at their brisket and just didn't feel confident enough in it. (I'd turn it in anyway, but perhaps that's just me.) So the number of judges on hand was always fluid.

Losing a judge, even one of the head judges, didn't mean the end of the contest.

"There's more," Cecilia said. She pulled up her phone and read from it. "'Henry Cargill is survived by his son, Darren.'"

They both looked at me, wanting to see when the penny dropped.

"Oh. Oh! I suppose that is the infamous, *angry* Darren from the slop house?" I asked.

"It is," Cecilia said, nodding. "I'd found out more about him. Seems that he, too, was a *troubled lad.*"

I rolled my eyes at her. The sisters just didn't have the right cadence to mimic my accent accurately.

"A few years ago, Darren was arrested for drug possession with intent to sell," she added, growing more serious.

"Is that where Darren and Timmy met?" I said. "As some sort of drug network meetup?" Did drug dealers have meet-and-greets?

"It's possible that was their connection," Gabby said. "Plus, there was that whole blow-up about his room being off limits during the summer scour. What if Darren was hiding drugs in there?"

"Was Timmy trying to steal them? Or find them, so he could report him?" I asked.

Gabby shook her head. "I don't know." She sighed. "I'm going to have to go back up to that bridge. See if I can get any more information from Timmy." She pointed a finger at me. "But I do not want *you* going back there."

I huffed at her. "I can handle a ghost." Since hooking up with Gabby I'd seen some things that were seriously off their nut. A ghost was honestly the least of my issues.

I wanted to be there for my girlfriend, to protect her, to keep her grounded in reality.

"I've been doing some digging into Samuel Montgomery, too," Cecilia said. "They found his body hanging from that very bridge. I couldn't find out why. The only article I dug up was much more concerned about how to cut him down than what put him up there in the first place."

"So everyone thought he had it coming," I said slowly. I nodded. "Right. So all of us should go. I'll go talk to my ghost. Gabby, you go talk with yours. And Cecilia will keep us grounded."

I pulled out one of the aluminium pans that we used for competition, grabbed the ribs and threw them in there, poured out the last of the spritz over the meat, then covered them with tin foil. I added more charcoal and turned to face the sisters.

"What?" I said. "The ribs will still be amazing, and you

57

know it." Instead of the three hours I'd been planning for the initial smoke, they'd only had ninety minutes. They'd be fine. Really.

"I said I didn't want you going back there," Gabby said.

"I heard you. I also decided that you were wrong," I said.

When she started to get that stubborn mule jut to her chin, I sat down in the chair beside her, taking her warm hand in mine, tugging on it until she looked at me.

I loved her dark eyes even when they were filled with anger and not passion.

"We all know that we need to solve this mystery sooner rather than later. Or we'll be stuck here all summer while you poke at it. And I'd like to win more contests this year than last year, thank you very much," I told her.

"I might not be able to protect you," Gabby told me softly.

"I promise to try not to get into a situation where you need to," I said earnestly.

In the end, both Gabby and Cecilia agreed that it was best if I did go.

Besides, we didn't have that much time to get stuck in some sort of ghost time loop.

I still had ribs cooking, that I would need to check in a couple hours.

# Nine

Absence had certainly not made my heart grow any fonder for that bridge. It was still a lonely stretch in the road, the place for cheating lovers and skewed promises. I didn't find the waters below lovely, nor did the cliffs hold stark beauty.

The deck of the bridge shuddered again as I stepped onto it. This time, there wasn't a handy car passing that I could blame it on.

Was the bridge actually moving? Or was it just me?

I hadn't thought to mention what had happened the first time to Gabby. I'd believed it had been caused by the passing vehicle. This time, I would remember to tell her.

Cecilia was the one who led us to the middle of the bridge this time. The walkway wasn't wide enough for two people across, so Gabby and I trundled after her like obedient little ducks.

At least it was still sunny out. I didn't want to visit this place on a grey day, the slick pavement threatening your footing. And possibly your sanity.

We stood on either side of Cecilia. She held one of each of

our hands, while Gabby and I placed our other on the stonework of the bridge railing.

That damned overlay showed up immediately for me. I wanted to ask Gabby if her hotline had rung up but I was too involved in my own personal drama.

Namely, Samuel being there, in my face, his blue eyes searing my soul.

*I suppose you want to know what happened. How I made such a wreck of my life,* he said. Or thought at me. Again, it was very disorienting, to hear the words so distinctly while his mouth never moved. Like trying to lipread anime or something.

*Perhaps,* I said coyly. *What I'd really like to know is what happened two weeks ago on this bridge. To Timmy.*

That earned me a snort. *Just another tragedy,* he said with disdain.

*Who pushed him?* I asked.

I really didn't care for the gleam that filled Samuel's eyes.

*Ah, that's the puzzle you want to solve,* Samuel said. *Well, there isn't anything free in this world. You're old enough to know that by now.*

*So you know what happened,* I said, wanting to make sure that I was going to get the information that I wanted.

*I did watch two individuals having an altercation,* Samuel said. *I can show that to you.*

That sounded exactly like what it was we were looking for.

*What's the cost?* Because while it might have been nice to go into the weekend with this already solved, I wasn't about to squander something important, not even for little Timmy.

*You just have to hold my hand,* Samuel assured me.

He held out one calloused, large hand toward me. Despite

the dust and the dirt embedded in the wrinkles, under the nails was surprisingly clean.

I didn't trust it, or him, one bit.

*What happens when I touch you?* I had to ask.

*I show you what happened,* Samuel said.

*And?* He'd said earlier that nothing was free. What was the price for this vision?

*I want a future favor,* he said.

*No,* I said. I willed my hands behind my back. My body didn't actually move, but I felt as though I'd made myself less available by doing so. *I'm not about to grant you an unspoken favor. I have no idea what you'd ask, or if it would even be commensurate.*

Samuel shrugged and withdrew his hand. *Your loss. Good luck finding it out on your own, though. That boy's not quite sane anymore.*

That made me fear for Gabby and whatever it was that she was getting herself into.

*Can you only haunt this bridge?* I had to ask before turning away. Had I imagined him speaking to me back in the camp? Or not?

*You know why they hanged me?* he asked in return.

*No, the article we found didn't mention that.*

Samuel's eyes blazed. *I was accused of witchcraft.*

I couldn't help the shudder that rang through me. I knew he was telling the truth.

Samuel had been a witch. Not only that, he'd had power. Here, now, when he focused on it, it radiated from him.

Normal people could only haunt places. We knew that a witch might be able to haunt another witch. But I wasn't a witch. So Samuel needed something more from me.

Gabby would be fascinated by this. There weren't many

witches in existence. She estimated the number to be about one in every half million to million souls. And many of them never found their path or figured out that they could perform magic.

As all the magic that Gabby knew about was elemental, people had to be looking for their particular affiliation instead of staring off into crystals or humming along in their meditations.

*Better go see to your girl*, Samuel warned.

I wrenched myself out of the overlay and back to the present. This time, the transition wasn't smooth. I had horrific vertigo and the world spun around me. I closed my eyes and held myself still. I was not about to sick up over the side of the bridge. We should have brought some water with us, though. As desperate as I was to help Gabby, I couldn't go to her right away. I rested my forehead against the cool stone of the bridge guardrail and took a few deep breaths before I could face the day again.

Had I gone deeper into that overlay this time? Was that why I was having difficulties? Or was it because I'd pulled myself out, instead of someone calling to me?

It was only then that I realized that Cecilia was no longer holding my hand. Instead, she was trying to take care of Gabby.

I pulled myself back together and straightened up, fighting down more dizziness.

What I saw wasn't good.

My girlfriend looked awful. Her naturally tan face was as pale as if it had been dipped in ashes. Sweat beaded up across her forehead. She leaned with her back against the rail, her head tilted to the side. Cecilia had both of her hands on Gabby's shoulders, holding her in place.

I stepped up as soon as I could, reaching under Cecilia's arm to take Gabby's hands in mine.

They were cold.

Cecilia registered that I was among the living again and shouted at me, "We have to get her off the bridge!"

"Roger that," I said.

The footpath wasn't wide enough for two, let alone three people to trundle along it. We sidestepped across, Cecilia in front with one arm under her sister's, me trailing with another arm around my girlfriend. Gabby at least made an effort to keep her feet moving, but we supported a lot of her weight.

Once we were off the bridge, Gabby took a shuddering deep breath in and shook her head. "Wait," she said.

Cecilia and I stopped tugging her along, though we still held onto her. Slowly, she found her feet, holding up her own weight, straightening herself up. Color crept back into her cheeks.

After one more deep breath, she opened her eyes, looking first at me, then Cecilia.

"Timmy is no longer sane," Gabby said after a moment.

That certainly wasn't good news.

"And he's grown stronger. Attacking the bridge," Gabby said. She shook her head. "It's only a matter of days now before something dreadful occurs."

I glanced back over my shoulder at the cold expanse that stretched across the river.

I did *not* want to go marching back across that damned bridge and demand that Samuel show me who killed Timmy so that we could fix this before everything came tumbling down.

I might not have any choice, though.

# Ten

Gabby and I sat together in the back seat of the truck while Cecilia got us to the campground. I kept my arms around her the entire time, trying to bring her temperature up. Cecilia had offered to break out the emergency blanket, but Gabby had vetoed it. There weren't any regular blankets, though Cecilia certainly had everything else one could ever have a need for: jumper cables, a long length of chain for hauling something off the road, a tool kit that was better equipped than my makeup kit, tissues, paper towels, and even rags.

Gabby finally stopped shivering as we parked. When we got out, she walked directly over to the UDS and stuck her hands on the front of it.

If any of us regular mortals were to try such a trick, we'd be in hospital stat with blistered skin and severe burns.

Gabby just gave one last shiver and straightened out. "You may want to see to your coals, Elanor," she said as she backed away.

I didn't know what she was going on about until I opened the small door at the bottom of the drum.

The charcoal had been transformed to ash. They still blasted me with heat, but I knew that wouldn't last long.

I got the fire rekindled and checked the time. I still had a bit for the ribs to be done, so I held onto my questions until I could sit next to Gabby, with Cecilia on the other side, and ask what that was all about.

Seemed that Timmy had been a bit grabby. He'd gotten ahold of Gabby and hadn't wanted to let go. He'd been trying to drain her power in order to break the bridge.

Now, Timmy didn't have any witch in him. Gabby assured us of that.

The bridge, though, had some level of magic that she didn't understand.

"I might be able to clear that up," I finally said, filling them in on my conversation with Samuel. I included the bit about how he could solve this mystery promptly. All I needed to do was promise him some sort of future favor.

"Don't do it," Gabby said flatly. "I can tell you're already thinking about it. I'm telling you right now. Don't."

I nodded. "Aye. I hear you. But what if it's the only way to get Timmy out of that bridge? Before it all falls down?"

"You're good at bargaining," Cecilia pointed out, "what with you being a lawyer and all."

I wasn't about to correct her that I wasn't a proper barrister, solicitor, or anything at this point. I may have graduated with a degree in law from Uni, but there were many steps that I would have to take before I could practice law anywhere.

"Samuel has had a lot of time to think about this," I said. "From our first conversation, he made it sound as though he'd been waiting for me. Perhaps he needed someone of our shared bloodline to escape that bloody bridge. He isn't about to be fobbed off by a mere deceit."

Gabby nodded. "If it's his magic in the bridge, so he's tied here, he's probably happy to help Timmy tear it down, so he'll be free. You're just an alternative option. Not the only one."

Gee. Always loved being told that I was merely someone's second string.

Cecilia glared between the pair of us. "All right. So we need to figure out who killed Timmy. Then what? Accuse them? Get them to confess? Take them back to the bridge so that Samuel can take his toll?"

I couldn't help the shiver I gave to that. "Think he'd probably ensnare them," I said after a moment. "The more the merrier to shake the bridge down."

The sisters both nodded grimly.

"Who is our primary suspect?" I asked. "Do we think Leticia did it?"

Gabby grimaced. "She was acting guilty at Timmy's celebration of life. But I also agree with Joan that she wouldn't have gotten her manicured fingernails anywhere near that bridge."

"So did Darren do the dirty work?" Cecilia asked.

"His dad did just die," Gabby pointed out. "Maybe Leticia prompted Darren to kill Timmy, then he turned on his father on his own? Supposedly killing people gets easier as the number of bodies pile up."

I nodded. While I wasn't thrilled that we might have a serial killer on our hands, that made the most sense.

"We need a reason to go talk with Darren," I said.

"I know!" Gabby exclaimed. "We make it some sort of official BBQ thing, and bring some food to the house of mourning."

Cecilia nodded. "There wasn't any mention of a wife or mother," she said. "I'll do a bit of digging on that, see if I can find a newspaper archive with a death certificate or a divorce decree."

Swell. Maybe little Darren had been extra busy, and taken care of Mommy Dearest first?

I looked sadly over at my UDS. When had grilling meat gotten so complicated?

The sisters and I were not having an argument. Possibly a heated disagreement about our next steps. But we weren't really fighting. No raised voices for this Brit. I'd been brought up much better than that. I fought with ice-cold disdain and biting sarcasm.

Gabby and Cecilia argued in a different fashion, more loudly, and generally with a dramatic flair. It had taken Gabby and I awhile to figure out how to communicate our anger to one another. Being yelled at shuts me down, while she stops listening when I get snippy.

I'm not saying that we got it right all the time. However, even when cues were missed, we could always call a truce and talk about it later. Making up was part of the fun.

The sisters wanted to take the beautiful ribs I'd just finished (and they had turned out divine) and bring them to the grieving family in town.

That sort of awkward social gathering just sent chills down my spine. Why would I barge in on someone else's grief that way? It had all the makings of a very bad sitcom but without the laugh track.

Being Mexican, the sisters had a different take on grieving, as well as the dead. They celebrated death, welcomed it, danced with it. It was part of the Las Chicas' logo. *Dia de Muertos* wasn't just a holiday but a way of life. Of course the family would want people gathered around them, a community they could cry with.

We English were much more private about such things. And none of us knew which take the Cargill family was going to have.

I'd just finished pointing out, *again*, that I didn't want to go where I wasn't welcome, when Cecilia looked over my shoulder and then had the audacity to *wave* at someone who was walking by our camp.

I turned to find Reverend Bob approaching.

Reverend Bob did barbecue contests fulltime during the summer months, heading up an appropriately named team called Holy Smokes. I believe he was some sort of school teacher the rest of the year. He was a fully ordained minister and had married more than one happy couple at a competition. In his mid-fifties, he had the appropriate laugh lines crinkling his skin around his mouth and the corners of his gray eyes. He kept his white skull fully shaved, though he sported a long salt-and-pepper mustache along with a rather natty goatee.

He was a bit more dressed up than usual, wearing a proper button-down that was white with subtle blue pinstripes and khaki slacks. Still had on his usual leather sandals, though. No socks, which I approved of.

Generally, I only ever saw Reverend Bob in his team T-shirt, that had the letters WWJG on the front with the acronym spelled out across the back, "What Would Jesus Grill?"

Part of Revered Bob's schtick, as it were, was to bless the smokers of contestants before the start of every competition. He'd fill a couple of buckets with water on Friday morning and pray over them off and on for twenty-four hours. Then he'd walk around the site, offering his services for free. He'd use a clean mop brush and fling drops of his "holy" water onto your grill while saying a short prayer.

We'd never taken him up on his offer. While Gabby had been raised to be much more of a believer than my CoE upbringing had left me, she still felt it was a conflict of interest as it were.

However, we were still friendly with Reverend Bob. Everyone was. He was a good, well-meaning bloke, who kept his confidences. Sort of the camp counselor, as it were.

"Greetings and salutations!" Reverend Bob said, giving us all a large smile. "Excuse me for interrupting and possibly over-stepping my bounds. But I believe I heard you mentioning the poor Cargill family. Is that correct?"

I stepped up, taking the figurative bull by the horns. "We were," I told him. "I just finished a test set of ribs. Absolutely amazing. Thought we might want to share them with the family, but we don't want to barge in or be a nuisance."

I glared at both Cecilia and Gabby at that. Because honestly, that was the true sticking point.

"I see," Reverend Bob said, holding his hands behind his back and nodding seriously. "Then you'll be happy to know that the family is welcoming visitors at this time. There will be something more formal on Friday evening, here at the camp-site, because a lot of the competition teams had met Henry at one point or another."

He gave us a large smile, having solved the issue for us.

I still didn't want to go, but I figured this was as good as the supernatural hotline ringing us up.

"Do you want to drive in together?" Cecilia asked.

That was actually rather clever of her. Hopefully, Reverend

Bob knew where the house was and could give us directions there.

"I'd be delighted!" he said. "I need to go wander back to my camp and pick up my own gift." He told us his camp number, and we agreed to meet him there in fifteen minutes.

I got my ribs sorted while Gabby and Cecilia stepped into the motorhome to change into nicer clothing.

It didn't really matter what Cecilia wore. She looked absolutely stunning in her white ruffled blouse and black slacks. She'd also applied a bit more makeup—eyeliner, blush, and a brighter red lip—enough to turn her look more formal.

I'd secretly watched some of her makeup tutorials on Clockticker. I'd read some of the comments as well. Seemed that while some of her followers appeared to be able to get the hang of regularly looking like a goddess, the rest of us mere mortals still struggled.

Gabby came out next. I thought she looked absolutely lovely. Then again, I always did. She'd also changed into a nicer blouse, though hers was off-white with peach and red flowers on it. It was subdued, for her. She'd stuck with jeans. She'd also taken the time to rebraid her hair, wearing it in a single long piece down her spine, weaving in peach and red flowers that matched her shirt.

It was my turn. I certainly didn't have any of my barrister clothes with me. I still had a rather nice gold, grey, and black shirt that I paired with jeans that were much cleaner than what I'd been wearing. (Seriously, I never understood how I managed to splash so much of whatever I'd been cooking onto my clothing.) My dirty-blonde hair held waves at the edges, mostly due to the humidity. I wore it shoulder length, easy enough to pull back with clips or a band. I also refreshed my makeup, though as usual, I was more subdued than the sisters.

My peaches-and-cream skin couldn't take a lot of color, not unless I really wanted to be tarted up.

Finally, we were ready. We all piled into the truck with Cecilia driving and the passenger-side seat up front empty and ready for guests.

Reverend Bob was waiting for us, his own tray in his hands.

We chatted about the town, making sure that Reverend Bob would know to visit *The Fish Palace* while we were here, telling him about poor Timmy. Gabby even suggested he go visit the bridge, see if he could bless it or something.

I wasn't sure if that was wise. What if something happened to him? Something supernatural? (Gabby assured me later that as he was completely mundane, none of the existing ghosts would touch him.)

Reverend Bob agreed to go take a look later.

Sooner than I liked, we were pulling up to a house on the outskirts of Starhaven. It was in a newly-built subdivision, with curving streets and plenty of cul-de-sacs, ensuring that a quick getaway would be impossible without a proper map. The houses had a bit of space between them—they wouldn't be begging a cup of sugar from their neighbors through their windows. The lawns were all manicured and monotonous. I'd never seen the point in such perfection. It wasn't as if the Yanks ever went outside and actually walked barefoot across the soft-looking greenery so desperately maintained.

Quite a few vehicles lined the curb. We had to park half a block away. (Oh the horrors of having to walk a few steps to reach your destination!) No pathways to ensure the safety of the pedestrians, of course. That might encourage exercise.

I still didn't want to do this. But here we were.

Gabby briefly laid her hand on my shoulder, as if to reassure me.

It wasn't going to be that bad. Right?

# Eleven

It shouldn't have surprised me to see Joan as one of the fellow mourners gathered with the family that afternoon. She may not have thought much of Darren, but she did have a heart.

In addition, Starry Smokes, another barbecue team, had already come to pay their respects. I learned that afternoon that they originally came from Starhaven. Their team were composed of two brothers—Kip and Felix—along with Kip's wife, Sharron. They weren't a fulltime team and didn't have a food truck. However, they were doing solid competition-level cooks and did have a line of rubs and sauces for sale. (Too heavily spiced for me. Their logo was a skull with stars in its eyes, which was supposed to represent just how hot their goods were. The sisters didn't like what they'd tried either, but I knew Starry Smokes did have their fans.)

On the way in, Reverend Bob was able to tell us that Henry Cargill's wife had left him a few years before, running away with the pool boy or something along those lines. She was not in attendance that afternoon. While she'd been notified, no one believed that she'd show up.

Darren was there, as pissed off as always. Surprisingly, it was not Victor who stood nearby but Robert, the sporty one.

Cecilia was the one to present the ribs, of course. Even Darren wasn't immune to her charms, and personally led her into the kitchen to show her where to stack them. Seemed the kitchen table was practically groaning with the food that friends and neighbors had brought by.

Hopefully Darren *et al* had a good freezer they could store all of that in.

Darren didn't appear to be feeling guilty. He wasn't too broken up about the loss of his father, either. Mainly he whinged on and on about all the work that had now fallen onto his shoulders. He wasn't sure if he could afford the mortgage on the house or if he was going to have to sell it. There appeared to be a lot of financial crap that he was going to have to clean up, at least according to him.

That surprised me. First of all, how did he know the financial situation so quickly? It would take time for him to gain access to the banking accounts, wouldn't it?

Or was he making assumptions based on what he already knew? Did dear-old-dad have a gambling addiction? Bet too much on the ponies? Maybe a secret online black-jack habit? Or did he have the equivalent of his own pool boy tucked away and living a life of luxury?

Though Darren's father had been a barbecue aficionado, Darren was planning on shucking all of his father's cooking gear. It was going up for a silent auction to be held back at the campsite on Friday. That was to help defray the costs of everything that Darren was doing for his dearly departed da.

Cecilia didn't have to ask the question about cause of death. Some neighbor did that when they came in.

Darren just snorted. "Death by brisket," he said. "Heart attack. Too much fat and cholesterol."

Gabby and I looked at each other at that pronouncement. Perhaps the police had reached their conclusion and had told the family, but it hadn't been picked up by the news yet.

Or was Darren projecting?

While Cecilia was busy pumping the angry boy for any more clues, Gabby and I spoke with Joan.

"I just knew it was going to be a horrible day!" Joan told us. "My horoscope told me that I needed to prepare for some bad news."

I nodded mutely. There really wasn't anything I could say to that.

"Did you know Mr. Cargill?" Gabby asked softly, pouring on the sympathy.

"Yeah," Joan said. "He and my mom were friends. When the Cargills moved to this place, he had a regular barbecue every month during the summer, that we were always invited to. Until Mrs. Cargill ran off." Joan gave a snort at that. "I don't blame her one bit. I met Alejandro. He was hot."

I was *not* going to be cheeky and ask whether or not Mrs. Cargill's horoscope had pointed her in the direction of her infidelity. That way led madness.

"Did Mr. Cargill actually die of a heart attack?" I asked. "I thought the police were still trying to determine cause of death."

Joan shrugged. "I know that's what Darren's saying. But the medical examiner probably would have required an autopsy, even if it was a heart attack, due to the circumstances. No, I still think it was something else."

"Like what?" Gabby asked.

"According to next-door neighbor Mr. Andrews, who

found the body, Mr. Cargill had been complaining of stomach cramps earlier that day. And he'd vomited. A lot. That might mean poisoning," Joan said.

"Did Mr. Cargill have any enemies?" I asked.

Joan kind of grimaced. "I'm not saying that people hated him. But people didn't necessarily love him, either. He was a stickler for the rules. Coming here to the BBQ parties always made me nervous that I'd put my glass down someplace without a coaster, or that I'd accidentally drop a bottle of some special sauce and he'd yell at me."

I will admit I had a modicum of sympathy for that. However, I'd also had the rules drilled into my skull from a young age, so I wasn't as concerned about making that sort of faux pax.

"What you're saying is that the list of mourners will be small," I clarified. "But was anyone angry enough to kill him?"

Joan shrugged. "I don't know. Maybe? Darren is pissed off enough to do it."

It was my turn to shrug. Darren seemed aggrieved by all the work that his father's death caused. I didn't know how angry he'd been before the death, though.

Though I'd had my fill of sticky sentiment and was ready to go, at that point, Leticia finally came swanning in.

I kept my sigh to myself, as I knew that both Gabby and Cecilia wanted a chat with her.

Like Gabby, she wore brighter colors—pinks and golds, with matching flowers in her long black braid. After she'd made the rounds, spending time consoling both Darren as well as Robert, Cecilia dragged us along with her as she went in for the attack.

"*Hola*," Cecilia said, giving Leticia a winning smile.

That surprised me. The sisters rarely initiated speaking in

Spanish to anyone. They never knew if the person just had a Hispanic look and didn't speak the language, or if they were ashamed and didn't want to stand out, to speak something other than English. (Albeit American English, but that's a whole other rant.)

"*¡Hola!*" Leticia said, visibly brightening. "*¿Ustedes conozco?*"

Cecilia introduced us and I followed along as best I could. I was somewhat fluent in the language, probably somewhere on the B level of the European scale, with A being the lowest and C being the highest. I could make myself understood in unfamiliar settings, but I still occasionally got hung up when Cecilia and Gabby were going full speed.

The sisters, having been raised in California since they were little, needed no help with their English. I still occasionally complained about the version of the language the Yanks spoke.

Apparently, Leticia barely knew Señor Cargill. She was friends with Darren and the others—Robert, Victor, and of course, poor Timmy.

I don't know why it felt to me that almost every word coming out of her mouth was false. She spoke pretty Mexican Spanish, and she spoke it fluently, natively. Like the sisters, she was truly bilingual, and spoke English with almost no accent.

However, something was off. I couldn't tell what, though.

Of course, she'd been devastated about poor Timmy. She assured us, though, that he'd been very troubled.

She went so far as to claim that she'd known that something was wrong. Yes, she'd heard him make some sort of promise to "that Joan girl" about dinner later that week. But she was the one who knew his heart. Knew that he was troubled. He'd spent some time saying goodbye to her that night.

She hadn't known that it was his way of taking his leave of her.

Of course, Leticia made it known that she'd gone to bed that night without a care in the world after dutifully saying goodnight to her parents, never imagining the news that she'd hear the next morning.

Eventually, we did run out of conversation and I was finally allowed my escape. Reverend Bob let us know that he was going to be there for a while and would catch a ride back to the campsite with one of the other teams who'd shown up for the impromptu mourning session.

I held back as long as I could, waiting until we'd at least shut the doors on the truck and started the vehicle up before I exploded.

"She's a lying liar," I told the sisters.

Both Gabby and Cecilia nodded.

"She was also very clever to let us know her alibi," Cecilia pointed out as she got us headed out of the labyrinth of the subdivision. "So while it's possible that she instigated the murder, she didn't do it."

"No, she had a partner in crime," I said. "But who?"

Gabby said quietly, "I know this is going to sound crazy, but I think it was one of the other boys at the slop house."

"Who, Darren?" I said. I was willing to consider that blowhard a prime suspect.

"No," Gabby said. "Robert."

"The sporty one?" I asked, wanting to make sure I'd heard her correctly.

"Yes," she said with a smile. "'The sporty one.'"

I snorted at her poor approximation of my dulcet tones.

"What makes you say that?" Cecilia asked as she navigated through the twisting roads of the subdivision.

Not that I had nightmares about being unable to escape from such places. Really.

"Did you see how he looked around the living room? Like he was proud or something. If I hadn't known better, I would have said that he was the son, the one who'd just inherited an entire new castle."

I thought back about our afternoon and had to agree with Gabby. "Good call," I said. "But what do we do about it?"

Gabby's phone pinged, indicating that she'd just gotten a text.

She smiled as she held it up. "Seems that Leticia has taken us up on the offer to meet this evening for dinner."

Swell. More peopling? I was just about done out.

"You don't have to go," Gabby assured me. "In fact, it would probably be better if you don't. We're going to be speaking in Spanish all night."

I sighed. "No, I can go with you. I'll keep up."

Cecilia caught my eye in the rearview mirror. "I actually agree with Gabby. I think it would be better for the Latinas to talk. We'll be able to get her to open up more."

"If you're certain," I said, though I really was happy about the off ramp for this social highway.

"We are," Gabby said, nodding.

"All right then, I'll spend the night whipping up a new sauce," I said. There were a few recipes that I had in mind, plus a flavor combination I hadn't tried yet.

Little Bavaria had had a marvelous spice market down-town. While we'd been there, I'd picked up some dried mango powder, as well as some sumac powder. I wanted to try a mango, sumac, and instant coffee rub, further sweetened with some brown sugar. Mango and chilies always went well together, and I had some *serrano* peppers that I'd already pickled that would add both heat and sourness. I'd have to dry them a bit for a rub, throw them either in the oven or on a grill, let them dehydrate some. Then what else should I add? Maybe some lemon peel? Or would orange peel work better?

I spent the evening happily experimenting in my kitchen, splitting my time between the oven, the stove, and the UDS I had going outside.

No ghostly voices haunted me. No one bothered me, though I did wave at a couple of other barbecue teams that pulled in while I was cooking, being neighborly and all that.

It was a lovely evening, relaxing while I practiced my craft.

I'd gone to bed long before the sisters came back. Of course I woke up when Gabby crawled in beside me. I asked her how it had gone, and she told me we'd talk in the morning.

So I slept well, feeling relaxed and loved, as all should.

# Twelve

I got the scoop on Leticia the next morning while we were eating breakfast together: over-night oats with some of the mango powder, fresh berries, cream, as well as a side of home-made bacon. It was a bit chilly that morning, and we'd agreed to eat inside the motorhome. We'd be eating outside every day after this, as there would be a lot of people walking by who we'd want to say hello to.

Seemed that Leticia was second generation. Her parents were from Mexico but she'd been born in the US. (The sisters were officially first generation, since they hadn't been born here but had arrived when they'd been children.)

As far as the sisters could tell, Leticia had just been stringing poor Timmy along, just like Joan had said. Leticia had "sampled" him, as she had many of the other boys. She'd referred to herself as the Queen Bee, with the implications of a bunch of mindless drones whose sole purpose in life was to pleasure her.

It made me relieved that I hadn't gone with them. I quite possibly would have stuck my foot in it (again).

"She also had some romantic advice for me, once I explained our relationship," Gabby told me dryly.

"Oh?" I inquired. "Do tell."

"Seems that there's a romantic spot just past the bridge," Gabby continued. "It's a gazebo that overlooks the river and the hills."

"A place for a lovers' tryst?" I asked.

Cecilia nodded. "Yes, and it's accessible both from the bridge side as well as past the tunnel."

"I asked her for more details about the spot," Gabby said, shaking her head. "It's remote, and you have to bring your own gear."

"So are we thinking that perhaps Timmy, though he was never in the Queen's Scouts, might have come prepared?" I said. "And left his gear behind in said gazebo?"

"Aye," Cecilia said. "And that perhaps we should go take a look-see. Then maybe contact the police about it."

"Right. Who's up for a road trip?" I said, collecting our breakfast dishes before standing and carrying them to the sink.

Gabby and Cecilia gave each other a look.

I put the dishes down then stood with my arms akimbo, glaring at the pair of them. "Look, we can drive to the far side of the bridge to get to this place, right? We don't have to park on the near side of the bridge and walk across. So neither Gabby nor I have to even set foot on that accursed thing."

"We'll still be driving across it," Cecilia pointed out.

"Samuel's only been able to contact me if I had my hands on the guardrail of the bridge," I replied. "Going across in a car, at speed, shouldn't give him long enough to be a bother."

Cecilia reluctantly ceded to my logic.

"However," I said, turning to Gabby. "I'm not sure you

should go. Our Timmy is very strong, and you haven't had to actually touch the bridge for him to get ahold of you. Right?"

Gabby nodded and looked pensive. "Could we approach from the other direction? Not from the coast?"

Cecilia pulled up a map on her phone. Turned out that while it was possible, it wasn't practical. The roads just didn't connect in a handy manner. We'd be two to three hours to get to the location, whereas by going down along the coast and then inland, it would take us only thirty minutes.

So it was decided that Gabby would hold down the home front while Cecilia and I would go scout out the gazebo.

While Cecilia looked like a goddess, I'd never really fancied her. Gabby had caught my eye and held it. So there was never any awkwardness between the elder sister and me. We only had a casual friendship, in part because Cecilia always held everyone at arm's length. She'd learned the things that her beauty could do to others at a young age, and so she'd started guarding her heart early.

Not that she wasn't a wonderful person. She was. But people tended to only see the outsides and fell in love with her looks, not working to get to know her.

The summer before she and Gabby had started their BBQ truck she'd had a nasty breakup. Though that was eight years in the past, she still kept up her guard.

So we chatted easily about this and that, the types and quantities of meats we'd be cooking for the contest, who the other teams were, how high she rated our chances at winning. Cecilia kept a spreadsheet of all the other competitors, as well as their general rankings. I frequently teased her about being a nerd, which she always took gracefully.

I will admit that I tensed up some when we turned away

from the coast and headed inland. It was just my imagination that the road ahead was covered with a haze, right?

Cecilia knew that for all my bluster about how this was going to be fine, I was nervous about crossing that bridge, even in a vehicle. She slowed down a little as we neared the cursed place, giving the car ahead of us time to pull away.

Then she gunned it and we shot across. The bridge wasn't that long. It wasn't quite blink and you missed it, but almost.

The vehicle didn't shake as the front wheels touched the structure. No ghostly voices called my name as we crossed. We were there, passing above the tumbling stream, then gone again, into the darkness of the tunnel on the other side.

I gave a huge sigh of relief and threw a reassuring smile to Cecilia.

"Nothing there," I assured her.

"Good," she said. "Since you went over easily enough, do you think Gabby could?"

"Possibly? While Timmy's grown stronger, and a bit grabby, I have to believe that he's weaker than Samuel," I mused. "He isn't a witch. Didn't come with his own power to the bridge. Samuel has to be feeding him. Which means that Samuel is the stronger of the two."

"You didn't bother explaining that logic earlier," Cecilia said dryly.

I shrugged. "Didn't want to worry anyone, be a nervous nellie or a bother."

Cecilia just rolled her eyes at that.

Just past the end of the tunnel was the exit for the gazebo. We climbed up a winding road that barely fit two monstrous American-made cars across, all the way to the top of a hill.

A very pretty gazebo stood there on a cleared rocky peak, with dark pines as the backdrop. It had recently been painted, a burnt-red color with gold fiddly bits and a black roof. At least it wasn't a "historic" site, but merely a pretty view. The stone marker that stood at the foot of the path was just an advert, about how this local group of do-gooders had paid for the rest stop. It also talked a little about the river below, which I finally twigged was called the Green River. Made sense really, given the glassy green color of the water.

Up this far above the tumbling waters the river looked prettier and a lot less tumultuous. The sound of it was also muted. The nearby area was filled with that lovely baked-pine smell that comes with summer outdoors. An occasional wind brushed against my arms, making the location seem chilly despite the sun beating down.

The gazebo itself had been built on an old-fashioned design, with eight sides. However, instead of being open, most of the walls were solid, with doorways and windows cut into them. The main openings had been cut into three of the walls, making them oddly spaced. Wooden benches lined the insides of the walls on three sides, again, a queer layout, unsymmetrical. It smelled of beer and pot.

A dark clump sat under one of the benches. I pulled on one of the sets of gloves that I always used when handling hot chilies or raw meat before I reached for the item.

Turned out to be a sleeping bag all rolled up. Stashed in the center of the roll were a couple of pillows and a half-dozen condoms.

Someone certainly believed they were getting lucky.

There wasn't a handy tag sewn into the bag that claimed it to be the property of Timmy. However, both Cecilia and I believed it must have been his.

Though the police had already closed the case, Cecilia still called it in. She gave them a whole story about how she knew that this had been Timmy's bag, and how she'd seen him coming up here with it the night that he'd supposedly killed himself.

The officer said they'd send someone up to the gazebo to collect it.

"Should we wait?" I asked.

"Naw, we don't know how long it'll take for them to arrive," she said. "And while I'm sure Gabby's fine on her own, you never know what trouble she's going to get into."

I snorted at that. As I said before, while I'm the youngest of the three of us, I was also frequently the most responsible.

And a fire witch, even one with good intentions, was more than capable of burning down everything around her.

We walked around a bit more, finding the very unofficial trail that led down the bluff for a short ways. It was steep, rocky, and all-together dreadfully dodgy. I let Cecilia go down that on her own while I was prepared to ring emergency.

Though the gazebo and its environs were a lovely spot for a picnic, I couldn't help but be glad when we were on our way again. Like the bridge, there was an echo of loneliness up there, a chill that no amount of sunshine would erase.

Cecilia wasn't able to build up a good speed on our way through the tunnel—she tried hanging back but the car behind us started rudely honking at how we'd slowed down.

The change from the dark tunnel to the bright bridge was abrupt.

I didn't think the bridge would be that well-lit.

It wasn't.

That damned overlay had shown up again. We plowed through ghostly workers as we careened over the expanse.

Samuel stood on the side of the bridge, watching us, his

architectural drawings rolled up in one hand. He raised them in a mock salute as we rapidly left the area.

I tried to tell myself that it was good to know that he could reach me even when I wasn't actually touching the bridge. To be honest, though, I found it more distressing than anything else.

At least we hadn't had to stay long.

I told Cecilia about it. And I told her that I was extra glad that Gabby hadn't come.

Who knew what sort of hold Timmy might have gotten on her?

# Thirteen

Though Cecilia kept checking her phone, she never heard back from the police.

She did, though, receive a mysterious text from Leticia, thanking her for doing her cleanup.

Then Leticia blocked Cecilia from being able to respond.

It wasn't until later that evening, when Joan came for a visit to the campsite (loaded with a few bags of chips, though no fish), that we found out what had happened.

Seemed that the police did go up to the gazebo to check out the bag.

However, it was no longer there. Someone had taken it.

*That* wasn't suspicious at all. Leticia had been the one who'd told us about it. Had told Gabby very clearly that she needed to bring her own supplies, as it were.

But the lack of evidence is just that. A lack. There was nothing to tie Timmy to the area, or to convince anyone to open the case back up and reinvestigate his death.

No, they'd need an actual confession from the killer to do

that. And even then, only if they thought it would be worth going through the mountain of paperwork that would generate.

We talked it out over chips that sadly only had vile American ketchup as an accompaniment. I was tempted to get out one of my own sauces but refrained.

The common consensus was that Leticia must have known that Timmy had laid in supplies, as it were, for their night together. Only she'd never intended on showing up. Instead, she'd sent someone in her place.

But who? Had that person been instructed by the Queen Bee to kill Timmy? Or just to rough him up, and had things gotten out of hand?

Joan assured us that the path across the bridge and then up the hill wasn't that hard to walk, though a bit steep in places. So it was possible that Timmy had walked up to the gazebo, dropped off his gear, then walked back down to the bridge for his "date."

"Who did she get to pick up the bag?" I had to ask. "I'm pretty sure whoever went up after us is the killer. And how did Leticia learn that we'd been up there?"

"She must know someone on the police force, someone who was willing to talk to her about our request," Cecilia said.

"That's a bit hinky," I said. "Also, not good at all."

I turned to Joan. "Does she know someone on the police force? Do you?"

"It's a small town," Joan pointed out. "Everyone is going to know someone on the police force."

"Point," I said. Village mentality and all that.

Not that I'd ever had a professor at Uni describe both the disadvantages as well as advantages of using said relationships at a trial. No, really.

"So Leticia knows that we're on to her," Gabby said. "I hope that isn't going to make it uncomfortable for you, Joan."

The bitterness of her replying laughter honestly sent chills up my spine.

"Naw, I'm good. She already wasn't my favorite person, and she wasn't a big fan of me, either." Joan sighed. "But she has an alibi for the night of the killing. You said she said good night to her parents, right? So they'll be able to cover for her."

I shrugged. "She could have snuck out afterward," I pointed out.

Cecilia shook her head. "Naw, I think she didn't do the first killing."

"What, are you thinking that she might have been responsible for Mr. Cargill?" Gabby asked. "Why?"

"Well, the police have now come out and said that he was poisoned," Cecilia said. "They made that announcement this afternoon."

"What was he poisoned with?" I had to ask.

"Anti-freeze," Cecilia said. "It has a sweet taste and can easily be hidden in other things. It's easy to acquire. It's also not that difficult to detect during the autopsy. You said Mr. Cargill had been sick that afternoon, right?"

Joan nodded, her eyes grown wide.

"Then someone probably gave it to him early that morning. Say, with juice for breakfast, maybe lunch," Cecilia continued.

"That means they'll be looking hard at Darren," I said, "since he has the most to potentially gain from his father's death."

"I know that Darren's angry, but would he do that? Actually kill his own father?" Gabby had to ask.

"Oh!" Joan said suddenly. "Darren can't be the killer. He

posted pictures on social media showing him and Robert cleaning out Timmy's room that morning."

"Was Leticia there?" I had to ask.

Joan pulled up her phone and started scrolling through her feed. "No," she said slowly, shaking her head.

"*Strangers on a Train*," I replied, nodding.

The blank looks I received made me despair, yet again, about the state of the American educational system. "It's a famous novel. Two men meet on a train and agree to exchange murderous favors for one another. As they are strangers, the police will never be able to connect either one with the person they kill. Of course, it all goes pear-shaped before the end. But I'm wondering if that's what we have here."

"Mutually assured destruction," Gabby said. "Darren killed Timmy for Leticia. So Leticia kills Mr. Cargill to get Darren from blaming her or bringing her into the initial investigation. They can't alibi each other, but maybe they don't need to."

"At the get-together after the death, didn't you say that Robert looked very proud? Was he also in on it?" I asked.

Joan gasped. "I saw that too! I was wondering what happened, why he was acting that way."

"How are we going to prove it?" Cecilia asked.

"We don't," Gabby said firmly. "We have to get them to turn on each other. One of them will break. Unless they're complete psychopaths," she added, turning to Joan for confirmation.

Joan merely shrugged. "Darren has always been angry. Robert—he's not the most real person in the world. And neither is Leticia."

"When did you first meet Darren?" I had to ask. "You were aware that he, too, has a record of drug use and selling, right?"

"Timmy told me," Joan said slowly. "According to him, they were going to keep each other clean and sober."

"I sense a big ol' 'but' coming," Cecilia remarked.

"But...Timmy had backslid, at least once, that I know of," Joan said. "He told me it wasn't going to happen again, though."

I shared a look with the sisters. We were all aware that drug users were like a cheating spouse, and that they'd be forever swearing to be clean and then breaking those promises again and again.

Poor Joan may have known the same, but clearly didn't believe that was possible with her precious Timmy.

"So how do we get them to turn on each other?" I asked. "And to do it quickly, because tomorrow is Friday, and we have a cook coming up the following day."

"We'll see them all at the silent auction, right?" Cecilia asked.

Joan nodded. "I'm pretty sure that at least Darren will be there. Possibly the others as well."

"Queen Bee wouldn't miss an opportunity to be out in front of her adoring public," I said dry. "She'll be there as 'support' for Darren. Don't know about Robert, though."

"If the three of them are in this together, then I think they'll all be there," Gabby said.

"Plus, there will be a potluck that night," Cecilia said. "Lots of free barbecue. Along with other things."

I grinned at that. I had already planned on bringing two things to the get-together: a spicy smoked cabbage salad as a cold side dish, then a chocolate dessert. Probably just truffles. I had picked up some dried apricots that I knew would pair well with a lighter chocolate, as well as the black currant curd (homemade, of course) that would be divine with a darker chocolate.

Joan wouldn't be able to attend; she had to work at *The Fish Palace* during the hours of the auction. And as she didn't close-up that night, she was going to have to close tomorrow night, which meant she wouldn't be able to visit until really late.

We told her not to worry, that she could see us Saturday morning at the contest. Gabby also gave her four free passes, two for Saturday and two for Sunday.

Anyone who went to barbecue competitions regularly learned that Sunday was the day to attend, not Saturday. On Saturday, all that the attendees could hope for would be restaurant or food-truck varieties of barbecue.

If they wanted to taste actual competition meats, they came on Sunday, and generally not until after the first turn-in. The teams would then sell samples of the leftovers from what they'd turned in to the judges.

Though Las Chicas de Carne had never been at this event before, we had been at others up and down the coast. There were some aficionados who would travel from contest to contest, showing up every weekend no matter where we were. We called them part of our BBQ family, even though they were just attendees and not competitors.

I assumed that we'd see some of them this weekend. So while we'd all be busy cooking, we'd also have more resources available to us if we needed information about someone or to have someone tracked.

A sort of "Scooby" gang, as it were.

Eventually, we said goodnight to Joan, with a vague plan in place.

Would it work?

That wasn't where my money was.

Instead, I had an over-under as to how quickly it would all go pear-shaped.

# Fourteen

While we were friendly with most of our competitors, we weren't what I would qualify as friends with more than a few. (The sisters had a different opinion, of course. Then again, they talked about making friends with someone after a single meeting, as if they were five years old.)

Fortunately, one of the teams that I truly did consider to be friends ended up right next to us in the campground: Alden and Zeek, who formed the A to Z BBQ squad. Though it was just the pair of them, they sometimes had the help of their friend Parker. (They were constantly making suggestions of names that Parker could use instead, all of which started with M or N, so that he'd be in the middle of the alphabet. He'd just point out, *again*, that Zeek's full name was Ezekiel, and until he officially changed his birth name to his nickname, Parker wasn't changing his.)

On the other side of us was the Diamond Grills team, made up of Finn and his wife Maribella. I considered them merely friendly, while I was certain that the sisters thought of the pair of them as bosom buddies. They were an older couple, and

Finn had very exacting standards when it came to his cooks, something I could respect. He was a data nerd, like Cecilia, and kept a strict ledger of his recipes and cook times. I often played more loosely with our meats. Sometimes that made us win big. Others, not so much.

Finn often bragged about his smoker, or as he called it, the "grillvette." It was insulated and painted a shiny blue metallic color. It also had a fan system that he had fully automized.

I don't want to tell you about the argument that Gabby and I got into the one time I suggested that we "tart up" Inez, our big smoker.

Inez looked as though someone had taken two big black oil drums and welded them together, forming one long drum. On the left side was the firebox, where the wood went. A chimney stuck up from the right side. Physics drew the smoke from the firebox out the chimney. While there were temperature gauges set in the two large covers, Gabby mostly controlled how hot Inez got through her magic.

Inside the smoker stretched long grills where I could place the meat. Two sets: one along the middle of the smoker, and an upper rack. Underneath the lower grills I placed pans filled with herb-scented water, to keep the meat moist.

Gabby always assured me that Inez had no magic on her own.

I was never certain that I believed her. Particularly since Gabby treated Inez like a person. Plus, I always wondered if constantly doing magic with a particular piece of equipment might turn it magical, eventually.

Gabby thought not.

Again, I wasn't sure that she was right. Inez had a glow to her some nights that at least to me didn't seem natural.

We put up the large banner at the front of our campsite

Friday morning, announcing the location of Las Chicas de Carne. We'd end up taking it down and moving it Saturday morning when we moved to the event location in town.

All of us would be in the campground on Friday night. Saturday night, while Cecilia would stay in the motorhome, both Gabby and I would be at the event location in a small tent, attending Inez and the cook.

It was fun to talk with the other teams, see how their latest contest went (if they hadn't been at the BBQ, Beer, and Brats event with us the weekend before, or even if they had been).

We were able to learn a lot more about Mr. Cargill as well.

As Joan had said, he was a stickler for the rules. More than one team had had run-ins with him and his interpretation of said policies.

Everyone agreed that turn-in times were sacrosanct. You didn't miss one of those. Not even by ten seconds. Standing in line and waiting to turn your cook in did *not* count. You were still disqualified. The meat had to be in the judges' hands by the end of the turn-in.

When it came to chicken, it was up to the individual teams what they turned in. Most used chicken thighs. Here, on the left coast, it was considered fine to use chicken drumsticks. I would go back and forth, using whichever one I thought would go better for that particular competition.

The contests that had delusions of grandeur got the thighs. For those that were more homey and welcoming, I'd use the drumsticks. As chicken was one of the last turn-ins, if we hadn't been to a particular competition before, I'd have to rely on what the other teams were doing.

Now, I was *not* shigging, a delightful term I'd learned when I entered into the world of BBQ. It basically meant going into someone else's camp and stealing their cooking process. I had my own cooking methodology, my own spices and rubs, thank you very much.

Part of what made me successful with chicken was the fact that I did it in the UDS and I timed it precisely, never opening the drum once to check on anything. (As it was so quaintly expressed to me once, "If you're looking, it ain't cooking.")

I'd figured out the best ways to build up a good head of steam in the UDS. All that moisture worked well with the meat, keeping it juicy and moist.

However, Mr. Cargill had made his opinion known that he considered anything other than a chicken thigh inappropriate. This had been awkward, as other judges preferred the chicken drumsticks.

In addition, Mr. Cargill always penalized teams that didn't add the burnt ends to their brisket box.

Burnt ends are the crispy bits on the edges of the brisket, where the bark of the meat is more heavily developed. It was *always* optional whether or not a team turned in the burnt ends. It wasn't required at any competition.

But at the contests where Mr. Cargill held sway, you had better put them in your box as well.

Nothing that Mr. Cargill did was actually according to the official rules, just ones that he'd made up. He'd even gone so far as to petition the LCBA to get them to change their guidelines. Fortunately, saner heads had prevailed.

It was later that afternoon when a trailer hauling a lot of equipment made itself home next to the large shared picnic area, where people could just come and share a meal—it wasn't for exclusive use of those camping.

As I was the one holding our purse strings, I was sent by the sisters to go and check out what was available for the auction.

I would have loved another drum—an ugly one, not one of those painted cans that came with a fancy fan system.

Our friend Lili worked with a company called TechGrill and sold the tarted-out drums. She'd offered us one at a good price, with a possible sponsorship attached, negotiation pending. While more money was tempting, Gabby was afraid such a fancy piece of equipment might make Inez jealous, so we hadn't considered it too seriously.

Of course, Mr. Cargill wouldn't have something as basic as an UDS. Instead, he had one of those ceramic cookers. It was roundish, and painted orange, generally called a Big Orange Ball, or BOB, for short.

A ceramic cooker would certainly come in handy for keeping things warm, holding meats at temp before serving. However, because they were made of thick ceramic, they were also really heavy. While I knew that some teams used them, for us, I decided that it would be more hassle than it was worth.

I was surprised to see that Darren was getting rid of Mr. Cargill's knife set. Then again, Angry Boy probably had no idea how expensive some of those knives actually were. The other BBQ teams looking at them all knew that those would be the best deal when it came to the auction.

The one I was eyeing the most was a cleaver. It was an Asian knife, with a beautiful wavy pattern on the metal and a sleek wooden handle.

I knew better than to even consider the big smoker. It had been well taken care of, cleaned regularly, probably with food-safe chemicals. (I was lucky in that Gabby took care of cleaning Inez.)

Then there was the entire table full of pans: Aluminium, tin, cast-iron, and others. The next table just held accoutrements, such as meat probes, forks, long-handled spatulas, peach paper (for wrapping brisket in), V-shaped stands for holding roasts, grill pans with small holes for veggies, oddly shaped cages that I later learned held whole fish, as well as scrapers and packets of steel wool.

I'd been curious whether any of the rubs or sauces that Mr. Cargill had on hand would be here. As none of them were, I felt certain that the police had confiscated them all. Which made sense, as he'd been grilling that afternoon and they'd probably wanted to test all the food stuffs closest to him for poison.

There really wasn't anything there that we could use. Sure, I would like a couple of those knives, a girl can never have too much high-quality steel in her life, you know? But everyone was eyeing those. No matter what I bid, I wouldn't get one.

For the silent auction, every item in the auction had little slips of paper with the number for the thing written on it. An envelope was also attached to each item, where people could put their names and their bids. The silent portion of the auction came first, everyone filling out their slips of paper. Then, while people were feasting on the pot luck dishes, some sad sack would be stuck tallying up all the bids. After everyone had stuffed themselves silly, the big-ticket auction item winners would be announced publicly, as well as how much money the auction had earned the poor, needy family.

Or in this case, that little liar Darren and his posse of murderous hobos.

Though I knew I wouldn't win, I still put in a bid for the cleaver. A girl could always dream, you know?

I dawdled going back to camp, chatting up some of the other teams I saw as I passed by. Lili was there, along with her beau Jason. They were both on the shyer side. At least until you brought up something about BBQ. Then, they would nerd out on cuts, cook times, and sauces like the rest of us.

While Cecilia was good at the internet and searching for information in all its nooks and crannies, both Lili and Jason were aces at it. They'd both been in that field before they'd started doing BBQ competitions fulltime.

It took a while to explain what had been going on. Now, they weren't superspy hackers, able to break into CCTV feeds and whatnot. But they did promise to find me every bit of information they could about Darren, Robert, Victor, Timmy, and little Miss Queen Bee.

I also mentioned that it appeared that one of the local bridges had been built by one of my ancestors. Why not sic them on Samuel Montgomery as well?

Very pleased with myself, I finally made my way back into camp.

Only to be met with dour faces.

"We have a problem," Gabby announced.

# Fifteen

I smelled the smoke when I entered the motorhome.

And not the comforting scent of meat being charred to perfection over an open flame.

No, this was a metallic smell. Burned rubber and wire. The kind that seemed greasy even if you weren't touching it.

Gabby led me to our poor meat fridge. Someone had pulled it out from the wall to get at the back of it.

The wall that the unit had been pushed against was all blackened. The back of the unit had been scorched as well. Just putting in a new mechanism to keep the box cool wouldn't be enough. We were going to have to replace the entire fridge.

At four PM on a Friday afternoon, in an unfamiliar small town.

"Did any of the meat survive?" I asked.

Gabby shrugged. "I can't tell. I wanted you to look at it and let me know."

I grimaced. The meat had to be kept at a specific temperature. If this were for a home cook, an afternoon BBQ sort of deal, I might take a chance.

But this was for a competition. Many, *many* people would be trying our products. I had to be one-hundred-percent certain that each and every piece of meat that had been in that box hadn't been exposed to too much heat.

"Okay, we need at least three more coolers," I instructed Gabby. "See if there are any we can beg, borrow, or steal from our neighbors. And more ice. I want to preserve what meat we can."

While we had a couple coolers, we didn't have enough for all the meat I knew was stored in the fridge. What I couldn't salvage or proclaim as safe was going to have to be stored in borrowed coolers or cooked that night.

Tomorrow morning, I was going to need to find an open butcher shop and replace what couldn't be recovered. In the worst-case scenario, I might even have to get some of our meat from a regular grocery store.

While I could make almost any meat taste amazing, the store-brand cuts took a lot more finessing. I'd probably have to change up everything, from rubs to cook times. Plus, it wasn't always possible to get fresh meat from a grocery store.

"I'm on it," Gabby said. "And Cecilia is already looking for a replacement fridge."

I was aware that some contestants didn't have an actual separate fridge or freezer that they used for storing their meat. They survived only on coolers and lots of ice.

I didn't like operating that way. Sure, the fridge took up space and we had to be careful about the electricity it consumed. (We used a spare battery pack to run it when we drove between contests. Best investment we'd ever made, in my opinion.)

I opened up the fridge, wrinkling my nose at the smell. How hot had the inside of the box gotten?

Even if the meat was still technically good, would it all taste like melted plastic?

Ugh.

I pulled out the ribs first, as those had been at the front. I looked around for a place to stack them, and decided that the little sink was going to have to do.

Before I could get much further, Gabby spoke up, startling me a bit as I'd thought she'd already left the motorhome.

"I don't think the fire was natural," she said quietly.

I lifted up four racks of baby-back ribs in my arms, cradling them as if they were an actual baby, before I tottered over to the sink and let them slide off.

"What do you mean, it wasn't natural?" I asked, leaning against the sink and facing her, giving her my full attention.

Gabby shook her head. "There was a trace of something else when I first touched the fridge. Something supernatural. The flames...fought me at first."

That put even more of a damper on my afternoon. My little fire witch had *never* had any issues dealing with fire before, not that I knew about.

"Was it a spell?" I asked. "Or a curse?"

Gabby glared at me. "You know magic doesn't work that way."

I shrugged. Gabby could only do magic in her personal area, not some fancy incantation. She could set things on fire, create some pretty cool lighting effects, or put out a fire. She sensed things happening far away. But that was about it.

And while she constantly assured me that was the way that all magic worked, I continued to have my doubts.

"So what was it?" I persisted, still standing there, staring at her.

Gabby pressed her lips together, as if she regretted bringing this up.

Fortunately, I could out-stubborn the best of them.

I stayed where I was, silent and staring, arms crossed over my chest.

Waiting. And refusing to give in to the guilt over just standing there when there was so much work to do.

Finally, Gabby spoke up again.

"The flame felt...ghostly. Lonely."

The only thing I could think of was that damned bridge.

"Do you think we have a poltergeist on our hands? Is Samuel trying to sabotage us?" I fumed.

"A ghost shouldn't have that much power here," Gabby said, shaking her head. "And Samuel, in particular, shouldn't be able to do anything in the RV. He's tied to that bridge."

"But he might have gotten into here," I said. "Through me."

I could still remember those ghostly words the night I thought I'd ruined a sauce. How I'd accidentally knocked over the hot spices.

"After I stopped the fire, it sparked to life a second time. Even though nothing was feeding it," Gabby admitted. "I put it down *hard* after that. It's not coming back. But it shouldn't have done anything after I touched it. Something else was feeding it."

"Something, or someone?" I said.

Gabby stared off into space for a moment, not replying. Finally, she sighed. "I'll go get you some coolers," she said.

"Thank you," I told her. "We'll get through this."

She paused before she walked out the door, catching my eye. "I know we will."

I shook my head and walked back to the fridge. Gabby had

no future sense, no possible way of knowing if we would actually be okay or not.

However, I knew we'd all fight to turn around our situation. And we did have a community to lean on, friends who we'd helped in the past, who would reach out a hand to us.

Despite whatever the bank balance might say, we were very rich.

Though the inside of the fridge hadn't burned, the pieces of meat at the back had cooked, the plastic of the sealed bags melting and forming hard, sticky puddles.

It was odd, and not what I would have expected from a fire that started on the outside of a fridge. Though I didn't get any ghostly or lonely sense when I was handling the meat, I knew this wasn't how physics worked.

I had the most hope for the ribs, which had been at the front of the box. However, when I cut open the packages, they still smelled of burnt wires, even after I'd rinsed them off.

We had absolutely no product that I could use for the competition that started tomorrow.

Fortunately, our friends kicked into action.

Though we didn't have much more than a passing acquaintance with Starry Smokes, Kip and Felix called the local butcher for us and talked her into staying open a little late so I could get some replacements for the competition cook.

It wasn't the best meat, but at this point, I didn't care. I just needed to have *something*. I'd have to work my own magic on it.

I bought brisket and baby back ribs there. I was going to have to look elsewhere for the chicken and pork butt.

Kip and Felix had some ideas concerning one of the big-box grocery chains in the area. Of course, they knew the butchers who worked there as well. I was able to get fresh chicken quarters that hadn't been packaged yet, so I knew they'd still be good. I pretty much bought the store out, as we needed to be able to serve something tomorrow to the general public, not as part of the competition. I also picked up some ground hamburger and ground pork, plus some eggs, planning on serving meatballs.

The pork butts they had weren't fresh though, and I didn't trust them.

Tomorrow, I was just going to have to go round to the various shops in town and see if I could find something usable. Or we'd just skip that category of meat. (I hated doing that. I always wanted to turn something in for every judging.)

I thanked Kip and Felix profusely for their help, which they just waved off.

"We know you'll be there the next time we need help," Kip said. "Or when someone else does."

I nodded.

Now, I wasn't about to go all wobbly-chinned at them. It still felt amazing to be supported in this way.

I only bought meat for that weekend. I didn't buy any extra for the next competition. The closest big town was Portland. They'd definitely have a good butcher in the city. And while it wasn't on our way to the next contest, we could still figure out a route that would take us there for an afternoon.

Gabby had organized coolers and ice for us, a place for me to stash this meat. Cecilia had struck out in terms of a fridge. I wasn't surprised. We needed equipment that would work with the motorhome. She agreed that we'd be able to pick one up either in Portland or nearby.

Despite all this, we were still able to make it to the potluck. My cabbage salad was a big hit as usual, and the chocolate disappeared immediately.

Some BBQers would tell you that all they ever ate were animal products. I'd been told in all seriousness once that chocolate qualified as meat. I never delved into their practices too much.

Darren, Robert, and the Queen Bee were all there. Leticia made a point of ignoring us, actually turning her back on us when we walked up to the group.

That was all right. We'd gotten a text from Joan letting us know that Leticia's brother-in-law worked as a deputy sheriff at the police department. We assumed that was how she found out about us calling in the sleeping bag, and perhaps that was how she got it removed to discredit us.

Darren was at least trying to be appropriately sad over the death of his dad, unlike the day we'd seen him and all he'd done was complain about all the work said death had caused.

Interestingly, Robert was the one escorting Leticia. Darren shot him dirty looks now and again, but kept getting pulled off before he could do anything about it.

"Looks like the Queen Bee has found herself a new drone," Gabby pointed out.

"I see that. And Darren is working himself up into a proper snit at this point," I replied.

Just what this potluck needed. A little drama.

Cecilia left Robert and Leticia on their own, instead, going up to Darren with her million-watt smile dialed up. She could light the whole area with just that.

Darren appeared happy to talk with her, particularly after making sure that Leticia was watching from a distance.

Poor little bee couldn't be in two places at once, though.

Many of our competitors had heard about the fire and came up to us, asking if there was anything they could do to help. Reverend Bob turned out to have some extra pork butt that he was willing to sell at a good price. So despite the "accident," we would be all right.

Until the next supernatural borking of our plans occurred, which I assumed would happen while we were cooking.

Despite what Gabby said, I *knew* that Samuel was behind our little fire. Though I didn't have the impression that he was a fire witch. No, if I had to bet, I'd say that he was an earth witch.

I had a little bit of understanding of what all the various elements did. Water witches could predict the future. Air witches dealt with the past. Earth and fire were firmly in the present.

But even if Samual had been an earth witch, there was something more to him as well.

Eventually, the auction scores were tallied up and the organizers got everyone's attention. Everyone had brought their own camp chairs, and so we all settled down to listen to the proceedings.

Darren got up and stiffly thanked everyone for coming, saying how much our continued support meant to him and the family. (His mum was nowhere to be seen. Rumor was that since she'd been cut out of the will, and as her alimony had just vanished, she couldn't afford to visit.)

Was it just my imagination or was that angry boy a little glassy-eyed? He didn't stutter or stare off into space too much. But there was definitely something off about him.

After Darren shambled off to the side, other people went up and said nice things about Mr. Cargill. I didn't know how much of it was utter lies. I figured at least half. Maybe as much as two-thirds.

Finally, the auction results were announced. The grand total was a couple thousand dollars, which Darren the brat tried to be grateful for. Everyone (not just my opinionated self) thought he was severely disappointed by the sum.

Starry Smokes got the big grill, while a team I didn't know got the BOB.

The knife set was split up between people, the lovely cleaver going to a good home with Lili. (Though I was certain that she'd sanitize it before using it, hopefully without ruining the handle.)

Unfortunately, we hadn't learned anything that evening. Our three main suspects were still on their own. The police didn't have any more clues than we did.

I wasn't feeling optimistic about us being able to solve this before it all came tumbling down.

Hopefully someone would have a brilliant idea come morning.

# Sixteen

I dreamed I stood on the bridge that night, on the end close to the car park.

The bridge itself looked similar to the other times I'd been up there, cold and lonely. The deck of the bridge bounced slightly with every car that drove over it. Dark sky above reflected the chilled setting below. Too many lights hid the stars. The roaring of the tumultuous river filled my ears. I could practically feel the freezing spray of water that it constantly spewed.

The whitish overlay washed over my view. However, instead of looking at the incomplete bridge, I was still in modern times. I could tell by the sleek lampposts and harsh neon of the lights.

A figure came walking down the path on the far side of the bridge. As it approached, I realized that it was Timmy. He had a goofy grin on his face, that of a guy anticipating a really good time later on.

Suddenly, a hollowed-out feeling took over my core.

It took me a moment to realize that someone walking from the car park had just passed through me.

Rude.

However, while Timmy was fairly clear in this dream (vision?) the other person was not. They were more like a rounded black ball of nothingness. I couldn't estimate their height, their weight, or even their gender from what I was being shown.

The pair of them met in the middle of the bridge. I drew closer so that I could hear them. Maybe I could identify the voice of Timmy's assailant.

But even when I stood beside them, I couldn't hear their words. Instead, it was as if their voices had been replaced with cartoon characters who'd been sucking on helium. They just made twittering sounds at each other. I couldn't tell if they were angry, overjoyed, or talking about sexy-times.

The black blob did strike the first blow, putting both hands on Timmy's shoulders and shoving him back.

Timmy didn't like that *at all*.

If this were a cartoon, he'd have black clouds of smoke and fire shooting from his ears.

He fell onto the other figure. They tussled back and forth, like drunken Grecian wrestlers.

The bridge bounced slightly, drawing my attention briefly away from the combatants.

A car started its journey across.

Some bastard (Samuel) had blackened out the license plate. But I knew (in that perfect logic of dreams) that I *would* be able to read those numbers in different circumstances.

When I turned my attention back to the boys, well, Timmy was just being tipped over the edge by his dance partner.

The act was deliberate. It hadn't been an accident.

Perhaps it hadn't been premeditated.

The result was the same.

Timmy took a swan dive into the river.

The black blob hustled away, back toward the car park.

I tried to step out of the way, but they still plowed through me.

I couldn't get a feel for the person. They were too firmly wrapped up in that cloud, obscuring their features, their scent, even their presence.

I woke in the dark, my little fire witch at my side. She snuggled into me, as if sensing that I was cold and needed to banish the chill.

While my body sucked in her heat, my soul still ached.

Samuel was teasing me with that dream, telling me that I could solve this entire mystery if I'd only give him a future favor. Not only that, there was also the possibility that someone else had witnessed the two people struggling on the bridge. Someone who could give their story to the police, who might then get off the stick and actually go and see that justice was done.

I didn't want to give in to Samuel's demands.

I might not have a choice, though.

The next morning after breakfast we took apart half of the camp. Inez got loaded back onto the trailer, along with the Las Chicas de Carne banner, the small tent that Gabby and I would share that night, as well as about half the cooking supplies.

Of course, we'd forget things and have to make more than one trip. Or rather, Gabby would. That was okay. I'd grown accustomed to the disarray that was Gabby when she was setting up a new space.

We drove into town, to the big park where the event was going to be held, the Starry Nights BBQ Competition. After waiting in line with everyone else registering with the officials, we got our number and went to set up our space.

It turned out to be a large rectangle, about the size of a small rugby pitch. The teams were spaced out along three edges, with picnic tables in the center, and a stage where the band was already setting up across the bottom of it.

As luck would have it, we ended up in a corner. Those could either be the best places or the worst, depending on how customers traversed the area. Either they'd congregate around us and we'd sell a lot, or they'd be more enamored with our corner partner and so would block all access to us.

In addition, we were far away from where the band would play, which I always counted as a blessing—country-western music tended to be favored at these events, and that had never been my favorite. Sometimes we'd get a band that did a lot of popular covers. There was even the one near San Francisco that had done mostly rap. We'd see what this weekend brought.

We set up our Las Chicas de Carne banner first, defining our space, before we hauled Inez out of the trailer, parking her across the back. Beside her, I placed the UDS. Then we popped open the canopy to provide us with some shade, readjusting Inez so she wouldn't smoke us out while she was running.

Tables went up next, along with all the serving equipment, like compostable paper bowls and wooden sporks, serviettes and chafing dishes. That meant the front part of the camp was pretty much finished. All it needed was some food to serve.

Turned out that my lovely fire witch forgot to bring fire-wood with us. (I had remembered the charcoal for the UDS.)

She drove back up to the campgrounds while I set up our tent out behind the public area.

Reverend Bob came by with his bucket of "holy" water and the pork butts he'd promised me. He was his usual scruffy self that I'd grown to expect at a competition, with his WWJG black T-shirt, shorts that would make any hoarder proud given the number of bulging pockets, and his usual brown-leather sandals.

"Thank you so much for the meat," I told him, handing him a check. "I really appreciate it."

He just grinned at me. His salt-and-pepper mustache was extra-long and droopy that day, giving him the appearance of a happy walrus.

"I'm counting on you giving me a run for the money in terms of the cook," he said seriously. "I know you're amazing. I still think I can beat you."

"Bring it," I told him with a grin.

"Would you like a blessing this fine morning?" Reverend Bob asked, hefting his bucket up.

I debated for a moment before saying, "Sure. Why not?" Gabby wasn't there, and I didn't think that Inez would mind.

Bob did his thing, flinging a few drops of water from his mop brush onto the black hulking beast before saying a quick prayer about letting all who came in contact with our food to know great satisfaction and peace.

It was really nice, even if I didn't believe in that sort of thing. Then again, I knew actual witches and magic.

At least he was well gone by the time Gabby came back.

I started up building a good bed of coals in the UDS, but we couldn't cook anything until the inspector came by. Fortunately, he reached us very soon after that.

After verifying that the meat was fresh and that our prep

area met the standards set for the contest, I was able to start cooking.

Into one bowl went my spice mix. While I always loved inventing new flavors and combinations, for a commercial cook that I'd be selling to customers, I needed to use the Las Chicas products that we had for sale.

For the meat itself, I used our Carne Carnival Rub. Honestly, it was mostly just your basic spices—garlic, salt, pepper, chili flakes, onion powder, smoked paprika, mustard powder, and rosemary. However, one of the things that made our rubs a bit out of the ordinary was that we used a powdered lime juice instead of the normal citric acid. It gave our rubs better acidic notes. (Not that I was biased or anything.) We also always used brown sugar instead of white.

Into the biggest bowl went the ground pork and hamburger, followed by the rub. I pulled on my gloves and thoroughly mixed everything together. Only after I'd gotten a feel for the consistency did I start adding eggs, one at a time, to help bind the meat together, along with a little bit of panko.

A while ago, I'd picked up what I thought were a couple of cast-iron mini-cupcake pans. Hadn't known those existed until I'd come across them at a jumble sale. However, at a cook, someone told me that they were actually takoyaki pans, used to make a type of Japanese snack. Each had sixteen indents, which meant I could smoke thirty-two meatballs at a time.

I melted a bit of tallow (made from brisket trimmings) into the base of every indent, then used a small ice cream scooper to portion out the meatballs. That ensured that they were all the same size, which meant that they'd cook evenly.

I had decided to feature three of our sauces. While we always carried enough product that I could actually use it at a cook, generally I just made up some fresh for the day.

First was the apple chutney glaze, which honestly was one of my favorites: apples cooked down in vinegar, garlic, chilies, and other spices. It was sweet forward, with a bit of a kick at the end. I watered it down some to make a sauce out of it for the meatballs.

The next was a spiced lime sauce, which had lime juice, brown sugar, vinegar, soy sauce, ginger, garlic, and jalapeños. It was much more of a savory sauce, while still being lighter than most tomato-based ones.

The last was a new sauce that I'd just developed, Mostaza Delight. I was planning on entering it into the Mustard BBQ Sauce contest held by the National Barbecue & Grilling Association at the end of the year. It started with mustard, of course. And it had the expected vinegar and chilies. But then I'd added a lot of unexpected sweet notes, such as coriander, fennel, and tomato paste.

One of the good things about going to contests was that I was able to easily judge my audience, seeing what sold and what didn't. And the Mostaza Delight had been a big hit.

Gabby came up to me while I was heating up two of the sauces on the camp stove. We only had a small one, with two burners, but I made do.

"How you holding up?" she asked.

I'd told her about the dream, of course.

I knew it was just my imagination that a permanent chill had sunk into my bones. My hands were warm. The sun shone down brightly on us—while it was a glorious morning, I knew that this English Rose would be melting come midafternoon.

But still, I couldn't shake the feeling of the cold lurking in my soul.

"I'll be fine," I assured her.

"That didn't actually answer my question," she pointed out.

I sighed. At least I'd gone into our relationship knowing just how stubborn my little fire witch could be.

"I'm worried," I told her. "I feel as though we're being pushed into a corner by Samuel. He's made it hard on us, and he's going to make it harder still."

"How?" Gabby said, her eyes gaining just a spark of flame, like two little diamonds in those dark depths that I loved.

I shrugged. "I don't know how he's going to bung up this cook. I just have the feeling that he's going to try."

Gabby shook her head.

"What? Supernatural hotline down? No sense of anything?" I asked.

"Unfortunately, while your so called 'supernatural hotline' has been silent, I also have a sense of impending doom," Gabby admitted.

I blinked, surprised. I hadn't expected her to say something like that.

"So what do we do?" I asked, lowering my voice.

I *really* didn't want the people on either side of us to hear that we were afraid it was all about to blow up in our faces.

"We don't cut any corners," she said seriously. "We pay attention. Someone is always here in the camp," she added. "We've been split into two parts, but I don't have the feeling that the RV is in danger."

"No, Samuel has his bloody sights set on me," I said, agreeing.

"Aye," Gabby said.

She came up from behind and gave me a hug. Though she was shorter than I am, I still leaned back into it, soaking up what comfort I could, as the road ahead remained unknown.

# *Seventeen*

It turned out that our corner "mates" were Albert and Pablo of Smoking Good Q. This was actually fortunate. Albert sold an entire line of rubs and sauces that had no nightshades—no chilis, no paprika, no tomatoes. He called it "Nuthin' But Taste."

The reason this was fortunate was that his customers and ours were *very* different. Don't get me wrong. He made amazing BBQ sauce. Instead of a tomato base, he started with rhubarb. While it didn't taste the same as any of the tomato varieties, it was still delicious and satisfying.

However, people came to our booth for the spice, the chilis and whatnot. They went to his booth for a very different experience.

We'd gotten friendly with Albert and Pablo when they'd attended their first LCBA contest a couple years ago (normally they did the KCBA events). Gabby had helped the pair of them out of a pickle at the time.

Seemed that the HOT Grill Action Team had been bothering them, and yes, the frat boys who'd made up the team were as obnoxious as the name suggested. Quite frankly, they'd been bothering us to some extent as well, making a lot of suggestive comments about threesomes and foursomes and what not.

Pablo had been able to confront the team about some hinky business, and while they hadn't gotten disqualified at that event, we also hadn't seen them on the circuit for the last year or so. Hadn't missed them one little bit.

Albert already knew about our fire the day before. I'd hinted that we were concerned about sabotage (though I didn't explain that the nature of it would be supernatural). He agreed to always keep an eye on our camp.

Pablo and his new boyfriend (Ben, I learned later) came in shortly after that to help Albert, and I finished up the last sauce, adding it to the chaffing pan out at the front of our setup.

I heard a distinct *creak* as I was walking toward the UDS. Didn't know I could move that fast, but had the lid off, BBQ gloves on, and was reaching for the pans inside in the blink of an eye.

Seemed that one of the hooks that held the grill plates in place had cracked in half. If I hadn't come back when I had, I would have lost all of the meatballs I'd been cooking in that batch.

"Damn it, Samuel!" I muttered as I yanked the pans out and put them to the side. (Fortunately, I'd already put out the wooden cutting boards as a place for the hot pans to go. Our cheap plastic tables melted immediately under steaming hot cast iron pans. Ask me how I know.)

I knew, *knew*, that this was sabotage. Those hooks shouldn't have broken or been weakened. I didn't feel anything ghostly or supernatural. Then again, I wasn't a witch.

When Gabby came back to the booth, I told her what had happened. I was still trying to redneck a new solution for hanging the grill plates in the UDS.

Sparks didn't actually fly off Gabby. However, I was pretty sure that her glare could have set anything flammable on fire.

"All right," she said as she threw some firewood into Inez, lighting a fire immediately with a wave of her hand. "Everything gets cooked on Inez this weekend." She patted the hulking black cast iron smoker. "She'll protect everything."

"Thought you said Inez doesn't have any magic," I snarked as I moved the meatballs into the already heating smoker.

"She doesn't," Gabby said, nodding as she closed the cover. "That doesn't mean she doesn't have a soul."

I never knew what to respond with when Gabby said stuff like that.

"Completely mundane smoker with a soul," I finally settled on.

"She isn't mundane! She's the most special *parrilla*," Gabby said, patting the already glowing hot cover.

I knew that Gabby was serious when she started throwing in Spanish words.

I didn't get it. It was just one of those things.

Lili and her beau ended up down the line from us. Since Gabby was guarding the meatballs, I walked down to see Lili. As she sold drum smokers at these events, I figured she might have some extra parts.

However, Lili was so horrified at what had happened to me (and that I'd almost lost what I'd been cooking) she insisted that we take one of her extra drum smokers to use for the weekend.

I did but didn't want to take her up on the offer. On the

one hand, I was curious about the fancy equipment. How did it compare to my UDS?

On the other hand, I didn't know if something would happen to it if I brought it into our camp. Not only did I have Samuel to contend with, Gabby (and quite possibly, Inez) might not be pleased.

It turned out that Lili wouldn't take no for an answer. I'd never seen her so pushy before. Jason rolled the model she pointed to and started trundling it toward the back of our booth before I could stop him.

I didn't really get a good look at it until it was delivered, with me stammering thanks yet again. Jason waved my comments away and left immediately.

"What's this?" Gabby asked.

"Uhm, Lili being stubborn about helping us?" I guessed.

Gabby crossed her arms over her chest and glared at it. "Well, at least the colors aren't neon."

She was right. Most of the drums that Lili sold were obnoxiously brightly colored, with neon green claw marks raking the side or yellow and red flames shooting out against a black background.

This one seemed almost tame in comparison. The background was black and shiny. However, the flames were warm colors, a range of burnt umber and orange-tinted yellows. The company's logo—TechGrills—was noticeably missing from the side. Instead, there was a blank space just above the fire.

A place where the Las Chicas de Carne logo would fit perfectly.

Had Lili specially commissioned the grill and just been waiting for the time when she could insist we take it?

I will admit to being a bit suspicious. However, running

Inez all day would tire Gabby out, and we really needed her fresh for the competition cook that night.

So I got the new drum smoker started. I could no longer call it a UDS—this new one wasn't ugly. It needed a new name.

Maybe I could refer to it as the PDS? The pretty drum smoker?

Gabby just snorted when I told her that, then made me reassure Inez that she was the most beautiful smoker of all.

The things we do for love, eh?

I started up a second batch of meatballs, dividing the first two pans into the sauces. It was a little after ten AM at that point, and the event started at eleven. However, chances were that none of the attendees were going to be eating a lot until noon.

I double- and triple-checked the coolers, making sure that they weren't leaking, that our meats preserved in them were still at the appropriate temperature, and so on.

Gabby actually made me haul the coolers out from under the tables and set them beside Inez. I wasn't sure why she thought the big hulking smoker would protect the coolers from supernatural shenanigans, but I was desperate for any additional assistance at that point.

For the competition, I'd decided to do chicken drumsticks. (No, that wasn't partially to honor Mr. Cargill's death. Really.) That meant separating the thighs off. I couldn't do any of that work until the competition meat inspector came by, and they wouldn't show up until one PM.

All of the meatballs that we'd sell that day (and the chicken later) were "bought" by customers using tokens that the event sold. We only had to get out the cashbox and point of sale tablet for when we sold our products, the sauces and rubs.

Having been to more than one of these contests, I anticipated today being the lighter of the two days. Tomorrow we'd see a lot more traffic and would sell a lot more of our goods.

That didn't mean I slacked on checking everything. Possibly obsessively. I knew that Samuel wasn't finished with us yet.

It was only a matter of time before the next disaster occurred.

# Eighteen

The event opened. We charged a single token for one meatball, but only two tokens for three. We might sell out of product earlier, but that actually wasn't a bad thing, at least among the competitors—being able to claim an early sell-out was a type of bragging right, quite frankly.

Most of the customers took us up on that bargain, which meant they got to try all three of the sauces. Sold more bottles of sauce that morning than I'd been anticipating. Nowhere near enough to make up for the disaster the previous night and having to throw away almost a thousand dollars of meat, but hopefully, we'd have some prize money before the end of the weekend.

Gabby and I kept an eye on the coolers and the PDS, making sure that everything was still working as expected. Cecilia had come down from the campsite at the opening cannon (seriously, these Yanks and shooting off their big guns). She'd dialed down her makeup from "stunning" to "merely pretty." In the smaller towns, we'd sell more that way. If an event was closer to a big city, beautiful worked better.

LEAH R CUTTER

The meat inspector got to us about one-thirty PM. He'd started at the booths closest to the entrance and had been working his way around the rectangle. We couldn't start cooking until two PM, so I wasn't worried.

Once he'd cleared us, it was time for me to break apart the chicken quarters, separating out the drumsticks from the thighs. I set up my prep space at the back of our booth and was just about to start to work when a loud groaning sound caught my attention.

This time, I didn't move quickly enough.

One of the sets of legs of the side table that held the chaffing dishes for the meatballs suddenly collapsed.

The dishes slid one after another to the ground, spilling their delicious contents out over the dirt. The sauces splashed up (possibly in an unnatural way) and covered Cecilia's bare legs, making her cry out in pain.

Gabby was there instantly, making sure that the flames on the cans of Sterno went out immediately. The front table didn't take any damage, so we still had all our samples and serving utensils.

It was just an absolute mess behind the counter.

I glanced at Cecilia's legs, then grabbed a roll of paper towels and hustled over to her, wiping the sauce off her skin. Angry red streaks remained on her legs, showing where she'd been burned.

She stood in absolute shock where she was, standing stock still. I finally took her hand and lead her to the back of the booth where I had a bucket of water. I was about to start washing her legs when she appeared to wake up. She took the rag from my hand and started attending to herself.

In the meanwhile, Gabby had been working on the mess. She shook her head when I came over.

"It's all completely ruined," she said. "And the sauces had gotten way too hot. I hadn't been paying attention to the flames on them."

I bit my lips. I didn't need to say it.

Samuel had sabotaged us. Again.

We got cleaned up. Albert had some burn cream that he gave to Cecilia. I threw out all the remaining meatballs and sauces. Luckily, I'd be ready to start cooking chicken soon.

We came up with a different strategy for serving that. Instead of using the chaffing dishes, we'd keep the chicken in the back. People would just have to wait a bit longer for their food. Gabby would maintain Inez at a really low temperature, just hot enough to keep the chicken warm while (hopefully) not overcooking it.

There wasn't much else we could do. Gabby felt certain that Samuel couldn't touch Inez or the PDS as long as she stayed focused on them. While we reinforced the legs of the remaining tables with extra pieces of wood that we were able to borrow from our neighbors, Cecilia drove back up to the campground to shower and change. We put up a "closed" sign on our booth while we regrouped.

One of the officials from the LCBA came up while we were still sorting everything out: Roberta Okigena, a slim black woman who honestly needed to take a few tips on makeup from Cecilia. That bright blue eyeshadow wasn't doing her any favors at all, and the scarlet lipstick was, shall we say, eye catching. At least her outfit was relatively tame, with a light blue T-shirt (was it supposed to complement the eyeshadow?), beige capris, and white sandals that had seen better days.

"I was coming to say hello, but it looks like there was an incident?" Roberta said, leaning over the front table and casting an eye across the back.

Gabby and I glanced at each other. I nodded and stepped forward, while she stayed focused on the grills and the meat, not allowing anything supernatural to mess with our fires again.

"You would have caught all the excitement if you'd arrived about ten minutes ago," I told her. "The legs on the table holding the chaffing dishes with meatballs just collapsed. We can't salvage a thing."

"Pity," Roberta said, shaking her head. She wore her hair in a cute afro that morning, teased out and poofy around her head, following along and shaking of its own accord. "I was looking forward to sampling some. You'd been bragging some about that new mustard sauce of yours."

"I'm sorry, but I can't risk serving anything that remained in those pans," I told her seriously. "The dishes all hit the dirt, and I'm concerned about contamination."

That at least got me a huge smile. "No, no, that's smart. I'm glad you're putting people's health first and foremost." She paused, glanced back at Gabby, then at me. "Cecilia not joining you this weekend?"

I didn't have to fake the shudder I gave her. "Her legs were all splashed with the sauces. She'd gone back to camp to shower and change."

"Oh!" Roberta said, her eyes widening. "I hope she isn't hurt!"

"Possibly slightly burned," I admitted, "but she's due back here shortly."

I never resented people coming up and asking about Cecilia. That would be like a streetlamp resenting the sun. We put Cecilia's charm and grace to good use every competition. And getting the LCBA on our side wasn't a bad thing.

I chatted for another few minutes with Roberta before I went back to work on the chicken.

"You know, I think she has a crush on my sister," Gabby said thoughtfully.

I snorted. "Half the people on the circuit probably have a crush on Cecilia," I pointed out.

Gabby and Cecilia had their own relationship, with its own quirks. Each had been jealous of the other at one point. They were much better friends now than they'd been as teens.

While the pork butts would take the longest to cook, the brisket would take the longest to rest. All of the meat was unfamiliar. I had the best quality I could afford, but it was all an unknown.

Because I didn't trust the brisket, I started on that first.

First, I had to trim off most of the fat from the two briskets. For the food truck, we never trimmed the meat as hard. However, the judges didn't want all that fat, and you couldn't cut it off after the cook. I saved all the scraps, of course. Would make tallow from that, which I'd use later. The meat scraps went into a pot for our dinner, the start of a stew.

Then I shaped the pieces of meat. I wanted the smoke to easily roll from one end of each piece of brisket to the other, coating them with delicious flavor. So I made sure that they were all flat with rounded edges.

I debated injecting the meat with a sauce. That was, quite frankly, the fastest and easiest way to tenderize such a tough cut of meat.

In the end, I decided not to. Instead, I did what's known as a dry brine. I heavily seasoned the meat with coriander, black pepper, oregano, fennel, powdered mustard, smoked paprika, salt, and other spices, then I wrapped them tightly in cello wrap. When I took them out of the plastic later, the outside of the meat would be wet, which was why it was called a dry brine.

Gabby and I discussed the cooking times and agreed on a five-hour cook, with a five-hour rest, then an hour prep for the boxes. As brisket was the second to the last to be turned in, at one PM the next day, that meant putting the meat on at two AM.

I turned my attention to the pork butts next. A bit more fat on them was acceptable to the judges, as it was a fattier cut of meat to start with. After weighing the butts and probing them to check for tenderness, I guestimated we'd need sixteen hours for them to cook, plus an hour rest and thirty minutes prep.

Gabby argued with me about that. Our last pork butts had been dry. She wanted a fourteen-hour cook, with a couple hours of rest.

The science was on my side with that one. When you properly rest meat, experiments have proven that the meat sucks back some moisture, making the meat heavier than it had been.

How much moisture returns depends on the type of meat. Chicken absorbs the most, followed by beef, then pork.

The other benefit of resting meat is that it loosens the tendons that have tightened during the cooking process, which makes the meat more tender. Beef relaxes the most, followed by pork, then chicken.

So resting a hunk of pork for two hours wasn't necessarily going to make it more moist. However, I gave in on this one.

To ensure that the butts were not dry this time, I pulled out my mad scientist's gear, which included a huge metal injector and goggles. I pumped the pork butts full of a mixture of lime juice, vinegar, soy sauce, ginger juice, maple syrup, Worchester, liquid smoke, and a touch of chili oil. Then I did the same dry brining technique with them that I'd done on the brisket, though I used a sweeter blend of spices for the rub, then wrapped them tightly.

The longer those two meats could stay in the brine, the more flavor they'd take on.

The butts were the last turn-in at one-thirty. Given our time estimates, that meant putting those on at about nine PM that evening.

Ribs would take six hours if I was putting them directly on the grill. They had a turn in of twelve-thirty. However, the briskets and the pork butts were going to take up most of the space in Inez. So I'd cook the ribs a bit longer, using the upper grill shelves. That meant getting up at four AM to get them situated.

I decided to finish up the chicken before I trimmed the ribs. When Cecilia came back, we would open up the booth again, but all we had available for people attending the event were our sauces and rubs, no meat to try or to sell, since all the meatballs had been ruined.

The chicken drumsticks were the first turn-in, and I'd cook those in the PDS. They needed sixty minutes to cook and very little prep before going into the boxes.

All the prep work for the chicken was actually occurring now, while I was separating the legs from the thighs. I had to make sure that each one was perfectly trimmed, with the meat all down around the end of the drumstick, the chicken skin covering it perfectly, and the bone nicely cleaned.

Finally, I was finished and ready to start cooking the next batch of the chicken thighs. They'd take sixty minutes, and I stubbornly insisted that I use the PDS to cook them. I needed to practice with the new smoker. It wasn't my usual UDS.

Gabby did agree to watch over the charcoals, though she much preferred the open flame of Inez.

For the chicken thighs, even though this wasn't part of the competition cook, I still turned them as though I were going to give them to the judges. That meant making each of them uniform with the skin stretched perfectly across the back. As I worked, I would inject them with a touch of liquid butter that had been seasoned with garlic and salt before I placed them directly on the grill.

Now, some of my fellow competitors believed in doing what they called "cupcake chicken." They used actual cupcake tins for the thighs as a way of ensuring that each one would be the same size and cook evenly.

Me? I had spent a lot (A LOT) of time training myself to butcher chicken properly. It involved finding the perfect knife (I actually preferred a wickedly sharp fillet knife) and a scale to make sure that I got them all roughly the same size.

Now, I could use my hands to weigh a chicken thigh, to make sure it was correct.

While I was finishing up with the last few, a loud clatter made me turn my head to the side.

And to slice the knife right across my palm.

I stepped back instantly, throwing my hand to the side. Though blood was now dripping everywhere, I hadn't gotten any on my prep station. Little miracles and all that.

Gabby had risen from her chair at the noise, walking over behind Inez. She didn't notice my situation until she turned back.

"How bad?" she asked when she came over to me.

We didn't have running water in the booth. I'd splashed some water from one of the clean buckets across my palm.

"Bad," I had to admit. "Possibly, like, stitches bad."

"Samuel?" Gabby asked, looking at my still bleeding palm and not at my face.

"Maybe?" I said.

Had I cut myself before? Sure. This badly? And thinking back about it, I didn't remember my hand being anywhere close to where the knife went. It was an odd cut, across the palm. It didn't really make sense.

Gabby and I wrapped up my hand, then I insisted on going to the med tent alone. The sisters needed to stay at the booth. We had meat cooking. Who knew what would happen if no one were there?

The medic understood that I didn't want to go to an emergency room—I had a competition to do! He also (eventually) agreed that he couldn't guarantee that I needed stitches. I wasn't about to spend the rest of the day at hospital, only to be told all that I required were a few plasters.

As long as I didn't move my hand or try to use it, the bleeding mostly stopped. So the medic wrapped it up firmly, getting me to promise that I'd take it easy and go to hospital if it continued bleeding later on that evening.

I considered our options as I made it back to our booth.

None of them were good.

Samuel was forcing me into a corner.

I was either going to have to keep on fighting, or agree to what he wanted.

Neither option felt very appealing.

## Nineteen

It turned out that Sharon, Joan's mum, had trained as a nurse before she'd gotten married and drawn into the family business. She volunteered to look at my poor hand.

We carefully took off the bandages. The bleeding hadn't fully stopped, unfortunately.

However, Sharon borrowed some superglue from Lili (honestly, that girl carried everything) and used it liberally to close the wound.

Did it sting? Yes. There might have been a few hissed cuss words that would have cost me dearly had my own mother heard me utter them.

That did stop the bleeding, though. Sharon wrapped my hand back up, doing a much better job than the medic in my opinion. Though I still couldn't really use the damned limb, at least it no longer felt compressed.

Gabby had moved the chicken thighs over to Inez while I'd been at the medic's tent. I'd wanted to do them myself on the PDS, but I was down a hand. We finally managed to get some more food to serve to our guests, charging them three tokens per chicken thigh.

Joan and Sharon got theirs for free, of course.

I spent some time chatting with Sharon at the back of our booth. She'd reluctantly come to agree with Joan that Timmy possibly hadn't taken his own life, particularly after Joan had told her about the sleeping bag.

"I was always worried about him," Sharon confessed.

"And him being with Joan?" I asked pointedly.

She gave me a brittle smile. "Aye. And that. Fortunately, Joan was always a bit too tame for his liking. Which saved her some heartache."

I nodded. That Timmy had hooked up with Leticia over Joan was just bad taste, in my opinion.

"I know she says that he'd given up the drugs," Sharon continued. "But you and I both know that sort of promise is easily broken." She sounded as though she was speaking from experience, but I didn't dig.

I asked her about Darren, Leticia, and the others. However, she didn't have anything more to add to what we already knew.

I knew that she'd been friends with Mr. Cargill, so I then asked about him.

"Joan told you we used to be part of the group that went to his barbecue parties, right?" Sharon asked.

I nodded.

"Henry wasn't the easiest man in the world to deal with," Sharon admitted. "He primarily invited us because of my late husband." That was when I learned that the mister had died a couple of years ago from cancer. "Henry and Jason had a running argument about the best types of food. Henry always swore it was pork, while Jason thought it was fish."

I could see that. It also explained the fancy fish grills that had been part of the auction.

"Henry was very demanding," Sharon said. "I'll also tell you that Betty, his wife, well, ex-wife, wasn't the only one with a wandering eye. Rumor has it that Henry also stepped out a few times before Betty just up and left."

She leaned closer before continuing. "Someone once told me that he was dating a girl the same age as his son."

I merely nodded, not saying what I was thinking.

If Mr. Cargill had such tastes, had Leticia also taken him on board as another drone? Was she the one who'd gotten in to see him early in the morning on the day he'd been killed? "Gifting" him with some juice, perhaps?

And was Darren aware of the relationship that Leticia had with his dad? If she had a relationship at all. It was all rather squicky, if you asked me.

Joan and Sharon left shortly after that, and the event closed for the day. I directed Gabby how to prepare the ribs: cutting the silverskin off the backs, trimming off the ends so the ribs were squared up, doing yet another dry brine for the meat.

Dinner was quiet, just the three of us still in the event space. At least I'd started the stew before I'd been injured, so all I had to do was taste it to make sure it was seasoned properly while directing Gabby to cut up and add veggies.

I'd made a huge pot of stew because that was going to have to see us through the night. We had our schedule for when to get up, and had set backups of every alarm. Normally, I would trust that when we fell asleep, a single alarm would get us up.

Today? I didn't trust anything to work as it should.

The pork butts went on as expected at nine PM. Gabby would spend most of the night awake and tending to the fires in Inez. She insisted that I try to get some sleep instead of staying up with her.

Normally, I might have tried dissuading her of that, but I was absolutely knackered. I didn't know if it was just the surprises we'd had that day, the cut across my palm, or something else.

I crawled into the tent, only to find that my air mattress had gone flat.

Of course.

Fortunately, that just meant I switched sleeping bags and curled up on Gabby's side. (She has a much lighter bag than mine.)

I didn't expect to be able to get to sleep right away—my hand throbbed, I was both worried and excited about the cooks, and I was afraid that I'd have yet another vision in my sleep.

The latter turned out to be true.

It was as though I was watching a movie of my life. We'd get called up to the stage a couple of times for this cook. Then we'd pack up, head out. I saw us arrive at the next cook.

Then disasters piled up on us. Gabby getting burned when the chaffing dishes suspiciously caught on fire. Cecilia getting into a car accident and destroying the truck.

And so on.

Before each catastrophe, I felt the ghostly hand of Samuel reaching through me and touching the world.

It only stopped when I finally went back to the bridge and gave him what he wanted.

I was still struggling with the bad things when a persistent beeping invaded my consciousness.

Brisket time.

I crawled out of the tent and immediately stopped.

The sky was *much* too bright.

Crap. Had I missed the two AM alarm? What was happening with the brisket? Had Gabby gotten the meat on in time?

I raced around the other side of Inez, only to find Gabby wrapped in a blanket, sitting there peacefully meditating. She opened her eyes as soon as she heard me.

"Good morning," she said softly.

"What happened to the brisket? Did you get it on in time?" I demanded, going over and wrenching open the covers on Inez.

Meat lay evenly spaced across the grill. Briskets closest to the fire box, pork butts at the far end.

"None of the alarms went off at two," Gabby said, coming up behind me and hugging me. "But I got the meat on shortly after that."

Damn it! This was bad.

I poked the meat. While I'd use a probe thermometer in a bit, I'd learned enough to be able to tell the doneness of a cut of meat based on how it felt when I touched it.

The briskets were still too tough for my liking. The pork butts as well.

"Can you raise the temperature a little?" I asked. I checked the thermometers on the covers. They showed the right temp, two hundred and twenty-five degrees Fahrenheit.

Gabby nodded.

The noise of the crackling fire in the box suddenly increased. I closed the lids and watched the temperature creep up to two-fifty, then hold.

We added the ribs to the smoker. Well, Gabby did and I directed her where and how to place them. I did manage to refill the water troughs under the grill plates on my own, then we closed Inez back up.

If you're looking, you ain't cooking.

While Gabby added more wood to the fire, I set about making tea. Or at least trying to. It was awkward with only one hand. However, I stubbornly wouldn't let Gabby help. I made her stand there while I told her of my latest dream.

"You can't give in to him," Gabby told me sternly.

"But what if he continues to make our life hell?" I said. "I don't want either of you to get hurt."

"You understand the chances of me actually getting burned by a fire are astronomically low, right?" Gabby said.

I nodded. The kettle had boiled and I was pouring myself a cuppa as I thought.

"I'm aware of that. However, it wasn't a natural fire. One of the Sterno cans exploded. You were trying to contain it. They have a jelly inside them. It isn't a regular wood flame."

"I can control those flames," Gabby assured me.

"Even when you get splattered with burning goo?" I asked.

Gabby pressed her lips together. Seemed she wasn't as certain of that.

"Want some coffee?" I said, offering to make her some from the remaining hot water.

"Yes, please," Gabby said.

We used an AeroPress for her morning brew, as it was compact and easy to clean. We had a more extravagant setup in the motorhome, but this was easier to use when we weren't there.

We stood silently for a few moments, each sipping our drink, contemplating the day.

"I can't forbid you from going to see Samuel," Gabby said.

"From trying to bargain with him. Just know that I think it's a really, *stupendously* bad idea."

"I'm not about to argue that. I also think it's bonkers to go," I said. "However, I don't think he's a regular ghost. I think he's something else. And I think that ignoring him is only going to continue to ruck up our lives. Until someone gets seriously hurt. Possibly more than that, even."

Gabby sighed and nodded. "I'm not sure what he could be, though."

"He's been haunting that bridge for a bloody long time without destroying it," I pointed out. "In fact, the last survey of the bridge showed it in proper working order. Right?"

Gabby nodded. Lili had found that out for us, something I had never thought to check—that there would be a government agency that regularly inspected the safety of bridges. They'd make recommendations on when a bridge needed work.

Whether the government officials who received such reports would pay attention was an entirely different ball of wax.

"So what's held him there? And has it changed his powers?" I asked.

Gabby sighed. Unfortunately, there wasn't anyone who she could ask about such things. Scary Grandmother, back in Mexico, might have a clue. (Gabby had met her and her sisters once. They'd come across the border to California for a visit. She'd disappointed all of them by not returning with them. They hadn't parted on the best of terms—some sort of large-scale all-out witchy fight. This was part of the reason why Gabby always referred to her as Scary Grandmother. Not a sweet *abuelita*.)

So our choices remained limited. And our time was running out.

# Twenty

The charcoal for the PDS started right up. I'd managed to carry the full water pans and get them into the bottom of the smoker on my own. Most of the meat was already resting. I just had to pull the ribs in a bit.

Gabby seemed a little listless, so I told her to go take a nap. She didn't want to go anywhere, not when there was the chance of fire. Instead, she wrapped her blanket around her and curled up in her chair, closing her eyes.

I was sort of glad for the time alone, quite frankly. I needed to pull apart this puzzle.

It still didn't make the most sense in the world for Darren and Leticia to kill Mr. Cargill. There had to be something more. Lili had assured me that the house would sell for a pretty penny. And Darren, well, it appeared that the angry boy had a lot of credit card debt. Would that be enough of a reason though, for him to off his poor da?

I almost snorted to myself. Of course it would be for some folks.

And Darren had the perfect alibi. No one suspected him of doing the deed.

Poor Timmy hadn't been premeditated. Though I didn't know for certain, I still had Darren at the top of my list for potential killers. He hadn't gone to that bridge by accident, however. Someone had told him to go. Probably Leticia.

Lili had gone through all of Leticia's social media accounts. She didn't have a job. Or rather, her job appeared to be getting other people to buy her things. Early on, there had been replies by family members as well, sisters who worried about the Queen Bee. However, those posts stopped occurring sometime after Leticia met Darren. (Maybe she'd blocked them? Changed accounts?)

Those two were bound together in a tight web.

Had Timmy known about Darren? I would guess not. And vice versa.

Perhaps Darren had found out about Timmy, and poor Leticia had gone crying on his shoulder about how she hadn't been able to get Timmy to stop bothering her.

Again, Timmy's flight from the bridge hadn't been planned.

So, Darren kills Timmy. Goes crying about it to Leticia. Who tells him what...she'll help him out by killing his dad for him? That didn't make sense either.

I knew I was missing something. But what?

Could we solve this thing, and bring Timmy some resolution, before the end of the BBQ contest? Or would we be stuck here, frantically trying to fix it all before that bridge came tumbling down?

I still had more questions than answers and my options were narrowing down to one very, *very* bad choice.

Chicken was our first turn-in that day, at noon. Luckily, the drumsticks had cooked perfectly. I'd used a savory spice blend, heavy on thyme, rosemary, and garlic, with a good bit of chili spice at the end.

When you took a bite, the skin was both a little crisp but at the same time, had melted onto the meat. This meant that when you looked at your piece, you could see teeth marks in the skin, which I considered one of the weirder judging criteria.

I'd spent most of the morning prepping the boxes we'd use for turn-ins. Like everyone else, we used recyclable, heavy-paper takeout boxes. (KCBA still insisted on Styrofoam for their turn-ins. We were much more environmentally conscious out here on the left coast.) All meat was presented on a bed of parsley. Even I occasionally resorted to tweezers to make certain that the placement of every sprig was deliberate and that the entire box looked like a piece of art.

The boxes with individual cuts of meat had exactly six pieces of meat. That meant six chicken drumsticks.

Had I cooked four times that many? Of course. We'd sell the extra to attendees of the event. But it gave me a good selection to choose from, to make certain that only the most perfect ones went to the judges.

Same with the racks of ribs. I would only give the judges six ribs from the three racks that I cooked.

Brisket and pulled pork were a little different. A whole brisket has two parts, the fat cap and the flat. For a competition, you typically only give the judges meat from the flat, and again, between six to eight slices, and possibly with some burnt ends.

I divided the fat cap from the flat before I cooked the two

briskets. This gave me four large slabs of meat that I cooked for the contest. Most of this would go to the attendees, after the turn-in.

For the pulled pork, it was supposed to be tender enough that you couldn't slice the meat. It would just fall apart. So instead of doing slices, you got to put a mound of meat in the turn-in box. Of course, it still had to look amazing.

Each box was initially judged on appearance. The head judge for a table would display the box to the judges at that table before serving each one of them a piece of meat. Then the meat itself was judged. Nine points were available for each of the categories: appearance, taste, and tenderness.

The tasting was all done blindly. We'd turn in a box to the people out front. Each box would be assigned a number before being passed back to the judges. No one except the judges who tallied up the scores at the end would know which box belonged to which team.

As the meat had finished cooking, and all I was doing was prepping at that point, both Cecilia and Gabby took the first box to the turn-in, Cecilia carrying it and Gabby as backup.

That turned out to be fortuitous.

I was shocked by Cecilia's appearance when she came back to the booth. Both her knees were covered in dirt and the palms of her hands were all scratched up.

Seemed she tripped while they were walking up to the turn-in table.

Gabby had caught the box before it fell and our hard work spilled out all over the ground. She'd taken a bit of time to make sure that the chicken was presented in an acceptable manner, that the chicken drumsticks weren't jumbled together but still separated out and looking acceptable.

Both Gabby and I knew that this couldn't have been a

natural occurrence—something supernatural had to have taken place. Gabby had felt a wave of something cold just before it'd happened. Plus, Cecilia was naturally graceful. I don't believe I'd ever seen her trip and fall. That sort of thing happened to me or Gabby, not her.

It appeared that Samuel's area of influence was spreading. Things could happen to people even after they'd left my presence.

I couldn't worry about that. I had thirty minutes to make certain that the ribs were acceptable. Then would come the brisket, then the pulled pork.

Cecilia managed to get herself mostly cleaned up, though she would wear gloves for the rest of the event due to the cuts on her hands. At least she didn't have to go to the medic tent or get any stitches.

I understood that this wasn't going to be the last time that Samuel reached out and made bad things happen.

I was going to have to stop him.

Without giving him my soul.

# Twenty-One

We didn't have any more serious mishaps for the rest of the afternoon. Perhaps Samuel had diminished himself when he'd tripped Cecilia.

Fortunately, he wasn't able to cast a pall over our booth. We had many customers, quickly sold out of every meat we had available, as well as sold many bottles of both our rubs and our sauces. We might, perhaps, have been able to break even at this event. The people running the event sold tokens for one dollar each. After event expenses, I estimated we'd make sixty cents on each.

Joan came by, without Sharon that time, though we were assured that her mother would be joining her later.

I loved watching her eyes grow comically wide as she tasted our food.

Yes, my cooking was that good.

I talked with her about our theories regarding the two deaths, but unfortunately, she wasn't able to shed any more light on what had happened. She still felt strongly that Leticia had been involved, but I privately had to question if that was the case or if that was Joan's envy speaking.

The day wore on. When Sharon stopped by our booth, she insisted on checking my bandages. She applied more superglue to my palm, though the cut had stayed closed and was no longer bleeding at all. (Thankfully, this time, it didn't sting as it was being shut either.) Then she rewrapped it, doing a much better job than Gabby and I had done earlier that morning.

I have to admit I was relieved when the band packed it up and they started resetting the stage for the competition awards.

At some of the larger contests, one-hundred dollars would be awarded to the top fifteen teams. As this was one of the smaller ones, only the top ten would get any money. The big prize money didn't start until the top three instead of the top five. And there wouldn't be a grand champion of the entire contest either.

I'd done my best on every cook, especially given our circumstances. However, it was all in the hands of the judges at this point.

Gabby, Cecilia and I set up our camp chairs in front of the stage. Many of our BBQ family was there with us, like Lili and Albert.

I will admit that I was shocked that our chicken came in fifth, given the mishaps and how the turn-in box had almost been dropped. Kip placed first in that category.

We didn't score great in ribs. Unsurprising, as I hadn't been the one to actually trim them. Gabby had done her best, but she wasn't the perfectionist that I was. So we were in twelfth for that, whereas Lili won.

Cecilia walked up and accepted our second-place prize for the brisket. I was happy with that. I'd worked really hard on that meat. Seemed that Gabby had gotten it on in time.

We didn't hear our names for the pork butts. When they emailed us the scores for the entire competition, I was shocked to see that we'd scored twenty-second out of twenty-five teams.

Something was going on. How could we have scored so low on the pork butts and so high on everything else? I was going to have to have a serious talk with Gabby about Inez. I know she claimed that Inez had no magic. Yet at the same time, Inez was her own person.

Maybe Inez had decided that she no longer liked cooking pork butts? Maybe they left her greasy and she needed to be cleaned better afterward?

At least with the second-place entry, we got five hundred dollars. That went a long way to off setting some of the expenses we'd had for this contest. We weren't operating anywhere near the black, but the prize money would certainly get us closer to breaking even.

Maybe the next cook would go better.

If we weren't so haunted by Samuel...

We spent time after the award show hanging out with our friends, chatting about the cook, congratulating them on their wins.

Eventually, we had to clear out of the area. It didn't take long to pull down the banner and pack up the truck, driving back to the campground and unpacking what we'd need for the night.

Fortunately, no one ever expected me to make dinner on the last night of a contest. We had leftovers to stuff ourselves with. I wouldn't start picking up cooking duties until the next night. And that was only if we'd decided to stay an extra night, and not drive immediately to the next site.

Gabby went to bed as soon as I got some food into her.

She'd been awake for quite some time and was having difficulties keeping her eyes open.

Cecilia, too, turned in early.

Which left me alone with my thoughts.

I didn't want to go to that damned bridge again. I didn't want to enter into a devil's bargain with Samuel.

However, I also believed the truth of the visions he'd shown me, how he was going to muck up everything we did from here on out unless I helped him.

He wasn't about to kill me, demand a blood sacrifice, or any other horribly dramatic outcome.

He'd said he wanted a future favor. I'd spent time considering how to limit his asking power. I wasn't about to just hand him my life (or Gabby's, or Cecilia's). I'd thought about the wording that I could use with him.

If I was going to go see him.

I sat in my camp chair outside the motorhome, wrapped in a blanket, staring up at the stars.

Yes, Samuel needed something from me. He claimed that I was just a second option, that once the bridge fell he'd be freed anyway.

I didn't believe him. Even if Timmy tore the bridge to pieces, Samuel was still going to be stuck there. He had enough power to free himself.

He just hadn't. Why?

Unfortunately, sitting there staring moodily off into space like some emo teenager wasn't going to get me any answers.

I was going to have to go back to that damned bridge, at least one more time.

# Twenty-Two

I was pleased that starting up the truck didn't awaken either of the sisters, and that I was able to drive out of the campground without any issue.

I did leave them a hand-written note, explaining where I was going and what I was hoping to do.

Again, I didn't expect to die that night. Samuel wasn't about to exchange my soul for his. Or if that was his bargain, he could tear down the damned bridge while a parade was marching across it as far as I was concerned.

I liked my life, and I didn't want to sacrifice myself for a bunch of unknowns. I'm not a martyr. Never have been, never will be.

The walk from the car park to the bridge seemed extra-long this time. Was it just because it was so late? Every other time I'd come through here the sun had been shining. Tonight, I didn't even have the glow of the moon to keep me company. She wouldn't rise for a few hours yet, and wouldn't provide more than a trickle of light from her sickle. Instead, I was able to use a torch that Cecilia had stashed as part of her emergency gear in the back seat.

Cold winds blew after I crossed the last pile of stones and the bridge revealed itself to me. The roar of the river below deafened me. Car exhaust polluted the area. I shivered, goose-bumps racing up my arms and dancing across my shoulders and neck. The metallic taste of fear flooded my mouth.

The bridge bounced in an unnerving manner when I first stepped onto it.

However, instead of the whole special-effects overlay, all that appeared was Samuel, standing near the midpoint of the bridge.

He smirked at me as I walked toward him. I'd say it wasn't a good look on him. It was, however, an expected look.

*Seen the error of your ways?* he asked in that ghostly way of his, the words just popping up in my head without his lips moving.

I snorted at him, regardless of how my mother had tried to train such a response out of me.

*More like seeing if you can be talked into doing the decent thing, instead of insisting on this Faustian bargain*, I shot back at him.

That earned me a cruel smile.

*Needs must and what not*, he replied.

I pounced on that. *So you do need me.*

Samuel appeared to realize his mistake. He narrowed those brilliant blue eyes at me, glaring for a moment, before he gave me a nod. *Aye. And you need me. Or I'll make your life a living Hell, until you lose everything. Your girlfriend. Her sister. Your place of employment. All of it.*

*You need me to pull you from this bridge*, I guessed. *You lied when you said that you could leave it once Timmy destroyed it.*

That earned me an indulgent smile. *No, I didn't. I will be free when Timmy takes this bridge apart.*

*Would you die?* I had to ask. *And if you go with me, you'll continue living?*

Samuel considered me for a moment before he nodded. *Not quite living. But not completely dead yet, either.*

I nodded. I'd assumed that might have been the case, that Samuel, like everyone else, just wanted to continue on.

*I can't give you an all-access-pass future favor,* I warned him. *If you insist on that, I'm walking away right now.*

Though Samuel tried to keep his face impassive, I could tell that me just considering this made him happy. Possibly ecstatically so.

*But that's what I need,* he said.

Brat.

*No. I will not do something against my ethics and morals.* I'd been trained as a barrister, and I understood the difference. *I will not do something that will harm the sisters or our livelihood.*

*I'm not some sort of monster,* Samuel said. Wasn't quite sure how he managed to sound so aggrieved in my head, without any sound, but he did.

*What are you, exactly?* I figured I'd ask, since the opportunity had come up. *You're more than just an earth witch.*

That got me a cocked eyebrow. *So you know about the main categories of witches. That's good. Most of the common information about witches isn't true.*

I rolled my eyes at that. An actual fire witch was the love of my life. Of course I knew that almost all of the modern portrayals of witches with the pointed hat, crooked nose, and green-colored skin were merely marketing adverts.

*There are witches beyond the elements,* Samuel continued slowly.

*That* was news to me. I couldn't say that I was surprised, though. Gabby had definite ideas about how magic and witchcraft worked, and while she was the expert, there was a part of me that never quite believed her.

Magic was bigger than that. Or maybe that was just me yearning for the unknown. Or wanting to believe the marketing.

*Modern day witches work alone,* Samuel said. *Back in my day, we didn't.*

*You were part of a coven, weren't you?* I had to ask, trying to contain my own excitement. While Gabby insisted that covens were as much of a made-up thing about witches as everything else, there just appeared to be too much historical evidence that that wasn't necessarily the case.

*Each of us, and yes, there were thirteen, all played our part in the circle,* Samuel said, nodding. He paused and appeared to consider his words carefully before he finally added, *I was the joiner, the one that melded our powers together.*

*What happened?* I had to ask.

*Story as old as time,* Samuel said, sounding resigned, as if he'd come to some sort of emotional peace. *Jealousy was the primary trigger, though. One of the others thought that I was growing too big for my britches. They told tales about me to a particularly rigid religious group.* He paused, shooting me what appeared to be a self-deprecating smile. *I might have gotten a bit too cocky,* he admitted. *I didn't stop practicing, and they caught me at it. Everyone knew what we were about. They'd just never been able to see someone perform miracles.*

I nodded. Cecilia's interpretation of the newspaper article had been that everyone knew that it had been witchcraft, so that wasn't "news."

*I fought them. Nearly got away. But one of my own coven bound me,* Samuel said.

I hadn't seen much anger from the man, but I did now. Those blue eyes of his grew ice cold.

*So they were able to hang me,* Samuel said. *However, I'd built this bridge. I had blood, sweat and tears already woven into its expanse. Plus, I was the joiner of things. And what is a bridge but something that connects disparate parts together? As I died, I was able to meld my soul into the stones.*

*Then what happened?* I prodded. I knew that wasn't the end of the story, of the problems Samuel had had with his coven.

He smirked at me. *You're a bright one, aren't you?*

I didn't comment, but just waited for his reply.

He gave a great sigh (though his chest never moved) before he continued. *I caught the souls of the rest of the coven as they passed, absorbing them into myself.*

That at least explained his power. However, it only fueled my suspicions.

*So are you still out to get the members of your coven? Go after their families?*

He threw me a puzzled look. *Why would I do such a thing? I have their power. I don't need anything else.*

Though I wasn't some sort of barometer when it came to people lying, I at least suspected Samuel was telling me the truth regarding that.

*Then what do you want me for? What sort of future favor are you looking for?* I said.

He shrugged.

I didn't trust it. That was too nonchalant, too casual for what I knew of Samuel.

He had a very good idea of exactly what he wanted. And for some reason, he couldn't ask for it right away.

So we bargained, this ghost on the bridge and I. Back and forth, throwing out clauses and conditions and deeds that would or wouldn't be done. I nearly walked away three times. He turned and left twice.

I didn't realize just how long I'd been at it until after I got back to the truck. It took most of the night, though.

Finally, we came to a bargain.

I'd perform his future favor given all the restrictions that I'd managed to apply. He'd show me who actually killed Timmy, as well as the license plate of the car that had driven by, so we could find them as an eyewitness.

In addition, he'd ensure that Timmy would be laid to rest, no longer haunting the bridge and able to tear it to pieces.

I only hoped that Gabby would understand. Samuel had assured me that he'd already attached himself to me, able to follow my very soul due to our connected heritage. Just how, I wasn't certain, but I believed him.

He and I were joined, and bad luck would continue to follow us if I didn't give him what he wanted.

*Pick up that rock*, he instructed when we finally finished.

When I looked behind me, I saw a rock a little bigger than my fist sitting on the pathway behind me.

It hadn't been there when I'd first arrived.

It turned out to be supernaturally heavy. It took both of my hands to lift it up. When I looked over at Samuel, he merely smirked at me. *Throw it off the side of the bridge*, he said.

I struggled to raise the rock up. It felt magnetically connected to the bridge. Grit on the surface of the stone at least meant that it wasn't sliding out of my hands, despite the weight.

Finally, I heaved the stone up, resting it for a moment on the guardrail, before letting it topple off.

The rock floated for a moment, as if held up by an invisible hand. Then slowly, it started to fall, swaying slightly back and forth, like a feather.

When the stone was about halfway to the water, it lost its magical abilities, and plummeted sharply into the river.

A huge plume of water shot back up, as if the weight of the rock had been real.

The entire bridge shuddered once, then grew firm under my feet.

*What in the hell was that?* I had to ask.

Samuel gave me a sharp grin. *That was Timmy's soul. You're welcome.*

I rounded on Samuel. *You assured me that Timmy would have a peaceful rest after this. I don't think sitting at the bottom of the river counts as that.*

Samuel rolled his eyes at me and waved away my concern. *Now that he's disconnected from the bridge, he'll let go of this plane. He will be at rest soon.*

*What do you mean by soon?* I pressed. Being stuck in a rock drowned by a river for a year or so was not my idea of a good, restful time.

*Two to three days,* he assured me. *Timmy will leave in a short while. He won't be able to stay here and haunt this place.*

I nodded. It wasn't an ideal situation, but it would have to do.

*One more rock to pick up,* Samuel assured me. *This one you must keep with you as part of our bargain.*

I turned behind to see a new stone sitting there. This one wasn't much bigger than a marble. However, it was oblong in shape, asymmetrical, with a pearly white surface that had been polished to a smooth shine.

*I suppose this contains your soul*, I said sourly as I picked up the rock. It actually was rather lightweight, though it also felt warm. He'd said that I would need to carry something with me, some mark so we would be connected.

*No, that's just an easy way to track you*, Samuel said. *I can find you without it, though. If you want me to help and not hinder, this makes it easier.*

*Do I always have to carry it on my person? Or can I just stash it someplace in the motorhome?*

*While I'd prefer it to be in contact with you at all times, in the motorhome will be fine, at least most of the time*, Samuel said.

I nodded and slipped the rock into the front pocket of my jeans. Maybe I'd get it made into a necklace or something so I wouldn't lose it. Naw, putting it in the motorhome made more sense.

When I turned to face Samuel again, that white overlay washed over the bridge.

Surprised me when I realized it was Robert who was swaggering across the bridge, not Darren.

The Queen Bee really had been busy with the boys from the slop house.

The numbers and letters of the license plate of the car driving over the bridge were burned into my memory. I knew that I'd have no trouble recollecting them.

Then it was gone. As was Samuel. I stood alone on the bridge, shivering at the cold that had crept in.

The bridge still felt as desolate as it had before. Freezing waters beneath tumbled in a roar. The sky had grown noticeably lighter. A small sickle of the moon hung on the horizon.

Had I just made the worst deal in the world? Or the best? Only time would tell.

# Twenty-Three

Gabby was up when I returned to the campground. She was waiting for me outside, next to the roaring campfire.

"I'm sorry," she said, jumping out of her chair and rushing over to hug me.

That relieved me more than I wanted to admit. I was afraid that she might reject me after I'd gone and made my bargain with Samuel.

She took me by the hand and led me to the fire, wrapping a blanket across my shoulders.

I told her everything, of course, while she held my cold hand in her warm one. She needed to know, to understand what had happened. I didn't hide anything.

She was fascinated by the witchy stuff, which I knew she would be. It made her thoughtful as well. "I think...I think that Scary Grandmother hinted at some of this. But I thought I knew better." Gabby sighed and shook her head.

"Is it time for a trip across the border?" I asked, only partially joking.

"I hope it never comes to that," she said earnestly,

squeezing my hand. "That's like, the ultimate last recourse. When everything else has gone completely wrong."

I nodded, a little curious but not surprised. I didn't have the full story of what had happened. Maybe someday she'd tell me.

Or maybe not.

"I can't sense Samuel on you," Gabby told me as I finished up my tale and handed her the stone.

She rolled it between her fingers then shook her head. "Nope. Not getting anything magical from it at all."

I shrugged. I wasn't about to toss the rock away. I knew the damage that Samuel could do.

My hope was that by making this bargain with him, he'd at least be neutralized.

Possibly on a good day, he might even help.

"So what do we do about Robert and Leticia and Darren?" I said.

Gabby pressed her lips together as she thought.

"We'll get Lili on the license plate, see if we can contact the people driving the car. Maybe one of them saw something," she said slowly. "As well as dig into Robert's finances."

I nodded. I'd been thinking along those same lines.

"And I'll have Cecilia drive me to the bridge," Gabby continued. "I want to make sure that Timmy isn't there anymore."

"You sure you don't want me to go?" I said.

"I don't think you'll stay awake long enough," she said gently.

I tried to glare at her, but instead, I gave her a mighty yawn.

"Go to bed," she insisted. "You need some sleep."

I nodded and rose. Gabby did as well, pulling me in for another long hug.

I put my nose in her hair, smelling the floral shampoo she always used, mixed with the faintest scent of smoke, as always.

I possibly could have fallen asleep standing there, but she shooed me off, sending me back to our bed. I collapsed onto the mattress, barely remembering to pull covers back over me.

Then the world was gone.

When I woke up several hours later my left bicep hurt.

Damn it! Had I fallen asleep on my arm or something? It felt really weird, kind of rubbery, as if it didn't belong to me anymore.

It wasn't until I was standing in the shower that I realized I had a mark on my arm.

And by mark, I mean a big-ass tattoo.

I know, I know. I'm one of those weirdos of the modern age who isn't completely tatted up. It wasn't ever my thing. Plus, if I'd ever gotten one my mother might possibly have disowned me. She certainly would have marched me into a medical center and forced me to have it removed.

It just was never worth the aggro, you know?

I now had a hangman's noose decorating my perfect peaches-and-cream skin.

What the hell?

*Samuel!* I demanded.

We'd set up lines of communication between us. His ghostly presence didn't suddenly appear. I did hear his voice in my head.

*You bellowed?*

*What is this?* I asked, pointing to my shoulder in case he had some question about what I was talking about.

*You agreed to wear my mark,* he said patiently.

*Then what the hell is the stone for?* I asked, thinking back. He had indeed said *mark* not *stone.*

Crap.

*Just to make it easier,* he said, again sounding patient. *What, you don't like my artwork?*

*It's a little grisly,* I commented. *What, you couldn't have made it into a pretty bridge or something? Why does it have to be a noose?*

*It is my death that connects us, not that stony prison,* Samuel said.

I closed my eyes and shook my head. *Just go away for now,* I said.

It didn't occur to me until later that I'd called Samuel when I'd been starkers.

Too late for any sort of modesty.

When I came out of the shower, ready to face the day, I saw that it was only eleven AM.

However, progress had occurred while I'd been having my princess nap/tattoo session.

Turned out that the license plate belonged to the Isleys, a couple of retired schoolteachers. According to their socials, they'd been out of town for the last few weeks and had just returned, and had actually attended the BBQ competition. They'd taken a selfie of themselves and their friends right outside of our booth when we'd been closed on Saturday.

When I texted Joan about it, she insisted that I go along with her to talk to them about what they may have seen on the bridge.

Great. More socially awkward conversation.

I did carry along a bottle of the apple chutney. Seemed they'd been wanting to try that.

The directions that Joan gave seemed familiar. It took me a few before the lightbulb clicked on: the Isleys lived in the same subdivision as the Cargills. Only when I asked did Joan let me know that yes, the reason she knew them as an adult had been because they'd also been invited to the regular BBQ affairs.

Hopefully the apple chutney would be adequate. Should have thought to bring a whole slew of products and let them choose.

I dutifully accompanied Joan up to the house, ready to jump back into the pickup at the first sign of raised voices.

However, Susan Isley turned out to be a lovely woman, full of concern about Joan, aware of what had happened to Timmy and how awful that must be. She and her husband had talked about going to the police station after hearing that Timmy's death had been deemed a suicide.

Because they *had* recognized both boys, Robert and Timmy. And they had seen them struggling together.

While it wasn't irrefutable proof, it would throw something of a spanner into the works.

On the walk back to the pickup, my tattoo suddenly buzzed, like a phone on vibrate.

"Uhm, excuse me," I told Joan, actually digging out my phone and holding it to my ear as if I were taking a call.

"'ello?" I said.

Samuel's voice actually came through the phone this time, instead of magically appearing in my head.

Would wonders never cease?

It was a bit static-y, and it sounded as though he was speaking in a tunnel. But it was actual words, which somehow made them less creepy.

"So it appears that Mr. Cargill is something of an angry ghost as well," Samuel said.

He sounded smug. Then again, in my limited experience with him, that seemed to be his natural state.

"What does that mean?" I had to ask. Great. Was there now *another* ghost we had to appease?

"He's a bit upset about, and I quote, 'that tart', who came to visit him the morning of his death. In particular, with the supposedly freshly-squeezed orange juice that tasted too sweet," Samuel told me.

"Did anyone see her?" I had to ask.

"Now, you don't expect me to do all the work for you, do you?" Samuel said.

I couldn't help the eyeroll I gave him, though I don't think he could see it. Thought maybe he could. Or at least feel how little I thought of his response.

"Fine," I said. "Thank you for the clue, by the way," I added.

I mean, we were in a relationship. May as well keep it on the sweeter side.

For now.

"Is there anything we need to do about the *señor*?" I said.

"No, I've taken care of it," Samuel assured me.

What did *that* mean? Was Samuel some sort of vampire when it came to other ghosts? (He assured me later that he wasn't, that he'd just loosened Mr. Cargill's hold on this plane, a trick he'd learned. Of course he offered to show it to me, to show Gabby, but there would be a cost.)

I dropped Joan off at her home, suffering another hug, before making my way back to the campground, only to learn of yet more developments.

Lili, or more likely, her beau Jason, had found a couple of "hidden" social media accounts. They weren't locked down, but they were under fake names.

Lots of pictures of Robert and Leticia.

Plus, one off-hand comment about, "Two down, one to go!"

Though we didn't know for certain, we all believed that Darren was now in the cross-hairs of this murderous duo.

Though I fretted about being able to make it to Portland to pick up quality meat and a fridge, as well as arrive in the next town by the following weekend, things happened relatively quickly over the next couple of days.

Someone (probably Cecilia) made sure that angry boy Darren was sent links of the social media accounts that showed Robert and Leticia together.

He came out guns blazing on his own social media account, accusing Leticia of the entire plan to kill his father. He swore that though she'd talked about it with him, he didn't think she'd go through with it. It was all just a big joke between them.

He also mentioned that she'd told him that she might be pregnant with his child. And that they were going to have to get married immediately.

Fortunately, Darren wasn't smart enough to realize that posting such things to social media was going to get you a visit from the police regarding your father's unsolved murder.

We found out from Joan that Leticia had also been picked up.

As well as Robert.

Since the pieces were all falling into place, Gabby okayed us to head out. Timmy's soul really had dissipated over the last couple of days, and no trace of him was to be found anywhere in the area.

The bridge was safe, for now. The next inspection would happen in five years. Hopefully, Timmy hadn't weakened or damaged the stonework enough for immediate repairs. (Samuel later confirmed that. He was proud of the work he'd done on that bridge—even if he had been hung from it—and hadn't wanted it destroyed. He'd strengthened the bridge as much as he could before vacating it.)

We continued to get updates from Joan over the next month, with Robert turning on Leticia and spelling out the bargain those two had made, with him taking care of Timmy, her taking care of Mr. Cargill, and the plans they both had for Darren. Who would have married Leticia for the fake baby, then been taken out of the picture, leaving the pair of them with a sweet house and a sweeter insurance payout.

Victor and Joan ended up together, opening up their own accounting business, though Joan continued to work weekends at *The Fish Palace*.

As for me? Well, I have this ghost who haunts me now and again. More like a damned cat, though, as he only sometimes comes when he's called.

Like I said before, I'm not a witch. Never will be.

Might I perhaps have my own personal supernatural hotline that occasionally rings up with juicy tidbits about whatever mystery Las Chicas de Carne is currently solving?

I might indeed.

Plus a future favor that would come due at some point.

# Additional Short Stories

⌘

I've written a couple of short stories about Gabby and Las Chicas. This will give you more of a flavor of some of the other barbecue teams that they consider part of their family.

Enjoy!

Albert loved barbecue competitions. Or at least that was what he reminded himself as he drove up the interstate, leaving Texas for Oregon, of all places. He was going to take part in the first year of the Salmon Wilde BBQ competition, organized by the Left Coast BBQ Association (LCBA).

Most *real* barbecue competitions took place out east, in places that had a true barbecue tradition, like in Kentucky or even Alabama. (Though honestly, did white sauce even qualify as a barbecue sauce?) Hell, even Texas had its own style of barbecue—plain salt and pepper, letting the meat and the smoke do all the talking.

Oregon? What in God's name did they have for barbecue?

Nothing that originated there, that was the truth.

However, here was Albert in his RV, hauling Betty, his long off-set smoker, up the highway, heading toward another contest. He was only in his mid-forties, so the long drive wasn't going to be too bad. Plus, the family member he most resembled was his Great Uncle Willis, who was still alive and kicking at eighty-four. Sure, it meant that Albert's lanky brown hair would thin out (more), his glacial-blue eyes had needed glasses since he was twelve, his white skin burned worse than bacon if he stayed out in the sun too long, and his chin had definitely receded some.

But he was hearty and hale and rarely ever sick. He'd take that for the win.

Might be the only thing he had going for him at this time.

It was true that Albert and his team—Smoking Good Q—had lost the last couple of barbecue competitions they'd signed up for.

Maybe more than a couple.

Things kept going wrong: Betty ran out of fuel that one time, Albert had used salt instead of sugar in a rub another

179

time, then there was the time they missed turning in their smoked meat to the judges by five minutes because the clock next to the smoker had been set wrong.

When Paulo, Albert's number one pit monkey, had suggested that maybe they needed a change of pace, to try a new contest, Albert had agreed.

Which was why he was barreling up the interstate at the end of September for almost three days, though he was making good time, heading to Hawksville, on the Oregon coast.

Albert always liked to get to a contest area early, to do one or two test smokes on Betty before the actual competition started. Never knew what the weather was going to be like, and that applied to every city he'd ever cooked in. Might go in thinking that since it was July in Memphis it was going to be warm and sticky, only to be drenched in hail and cold. Or be prepared for frost in Kentucky in October, and be stuck in a heatwave.

Since Hawksville was a coastal town, Albert assumed humidity and wind, but that might not be the case. Maybe the contest itself wasn't in sight of the water, was set inland a ways, so was warmer and drier. But it was also the end of September, so who knew how much rain they'd get?

It didn't matter. This time, Albert was going to win at least one category in a contest. Bring home another trophy for the food truck he ran in Dallas. Albert had joked about getting a second truck just to hold the trophies and ribbons. Though some of his crew had warned about that bringing bad luck, it hadn't. Not for the first five years.

Not until recently, when his winning streak had stopped.

Albert shook himself, staring out at the highway as the old RV ate up the miles. Normally, he traveled with at least one other member of his crew. However, Paulo was already on location, as he'd gone up early. Had family in the area, or something. They'd drive back together.

Everything had to go right this time. They didn't have their usual group of onlookers to cheer them on, as none of their regular barbecue family was making this long drive.

Nope. It was just Albert and Paulo. Men against meat.

Despite the name, the Salmon Wilde BBQ contest didn't have a fish category. Instead, they'd chosen to do the traditional four meats of barbecue competitions: brisket, pork shoulder, ribs, and chicken.

Albert wasn't going to fuss too much with the chicken. He regularly made the top ten in that category, frequently snagging one of the top three spots that came with a trophy and a cash prize. Chicken was hard to do correctly, with the pieces uniform, the skin perfectly tender and melting into the meat, everything juicy and flavorful.

He didn't bother doing in the truck, just at competitions.

Ribs could also be finicky, but Albert had had good success in the past with those meats, often placing and occasionally winning contests.

Pork shoulder and brisket were his specialties. He had the perfect injection for his brisket that enhanced the meat flavor. Most competition cooks injected their pork as well, but Albert didn't. His rub and his cooking techniques were good enough that he didn't need to. He almost always placed high in those categories.

Except for recently, when all his tried-and-true recipes had failed him.

What he really needed right now as a win.

Hopefully, Oregon would get him back on his streak again.

The campground next to the park where the barbecue contest was being held was beautiful. Albert had no other words to describe it. Instead of a bare open space with concrete and each RV parked within two feet of its neighbor, all the campsites were tucked away under huge pine trees. The crisp air smelled like baked earth, with a hint of the ocean underneath. The weather forecast predicted sunshine all through the weekend— Albert had arrived on Thursday night, and the contest didn't really start until Saturday. But weather was changeable, and those people who predicted it had a lousy average most of the time.

Albert texted Paulo that he'd arrived, let him know the campsite he'd been assigned, then went to take care of Betty.

Betty was a long, offset smoker. She looked as though someone had taken three large oil barrels, laid them on their sides, then riveted them together. Hanging off the left side of the long metal body was the firebox, for the wood Albert burned. (Hence, offset, as the heat wasn't directly in the main cooking body.) On the right side, a large chimney jutted out. Sturdy legs with heavy-duty wheels supported the entire structure.

Each of the three barrels had lid as well as a built-in thermometer. Albert knew Betty well, where her hot and cold spots were, the best places to cook a particular cut of meat, how to get exactly the right amount of heat and smoke.

Generally, underneath the main grate that took up most of the interior, he stuck a large pan filled with water, to ensure moisture throughout the entire offset.

That afternoon, Albert left Betty up on her trailer, as he was going to have to haul her to the competition area Saturday morning, which was in the park just across the street from the campground. The LCBA had sold tickets to the locals, for

Saturday and Sunday, promising real barbecue. There'd be a band playing both Saturday and Sunday, and a number of local breweries would also have stands, mixed in between the barbecue establishments.

Albert stoked up the wood in Betty's fire box, getting a nice burn going, letting the smoker heat up before he put on his dinner—porkchops and baked apples. The meat had a rub of his own making, with lavender, rosemary, lemon peel, coarse salt and black pepper. Toward the end of the cook, he also threw on sauerkraut—store bought, but warming it up on Betty made it amazing.

Sure, it was a bit much, heating up the long smoker just for a short while. However, he wanted to make sure she was all right after the long haul. Plus, a short cook like pork chops was a good test for how she'd handle in this location.

Albert had managed to stay friends with his ex-wife, even after she remarried and started popping out kids. (It had been one of the reasons why they'd gotten a divorce—Albert honestly couldn't stand kids, and Rebecca had wanted a slew of them.)

One of her girls had turned out to be allergic to onions and garlic. Albert would have just as soon stopped living if he'd had to give up such flavors.

However, when Rebecca had challenged him to create something for Patricia, Albert had risen to the occasion and upped his spice game. Now, he frequently made his rubs that didn't contain the usual ingredients.

So at times like this, he experimented. He'd started adding lavender as a way to increase the lightness of a rub—what some snootily called the floral notes. Cloves were another of his secret ingredients: they added the earthiness of pepper without the heat.

The pork was perfect when he pulled it off the grill. Seared and tender, with just a kiss of smoke. The apples were fantastic as well. He'd done two of them, cored out and wrapped in tinfoil: one savory, with rosemary, thyme, and sage, while the other was sweet, stuffed with brown sugar and cinnamon. Plus, both had a generous serving of butter melted with all the other goodness.

Albert ate alone at his park-provided picnic table instead of inside his RV, enjoying being outside for the time being. The evening had turned much colder as the sun set. Some brave cicadas still sang in the grass off to the side. Maybe if it grew quiet enough he'd be able to hear the ocean off in the distance.

After he finished his stupendous meal, he poured himself a shot of whiskey and added it to his decaf coffee, wishing for the moment that maybe he had some hot chocolate instead. He tended not to like things that were too sweet, which was why he didn't have any.

It was so peaceful up here, out in the woods. Albert could feel himself recharging after three long-ass days of driving.

And Betty was working great after all that travel. So well, in fact, he couldn't imagine losing. Not this time. Not in this place.

Nope. That losing streak of his was over.

Paulo showed up midafternoon on Friday. He looked happier than he had been, down in Texas, his dark brown eyes softer, his grin wider. Even his dark Hispanic skin seemed lighter. He wore his usual stuffy, long-sleeved shirt, looking like a businessman, with a blue bandana holding his dark curls back.

"Hey, stranger," Albert said as opened the door to the RV when Paulo knocked.

"Howdy, boss," Paulo said with a grin. "See you got all set up."

"Yup," Albert said. He'd brought more than one grill, of course. While last night had been Betty's turn, this morning he'd started up the barrel smoker and made himself a slew of eggs and sausages, with a little of the sauerkraut from the night before thrown in, plus cheese, of course.

The barrel smoker was made from a single, modified barrel that stood upright. The bottom of it had a drawer that could be easily slid out for adding more charcoal or wood. Just above that was a second drawer that held a water pan. Then there were three layers of wire racks for smoking. The removable top of it was flat, with a chimney sticking out of the middle of it.

Albert's barrel smoker was painted black, with flames at the bottom of it and his logo—Smoking Good Q—on the side, just below the thermometer. The smoker was good advertisement, and it made really good meat. Plus, the guys who'd made it were sponsors of Albert, so the smoker itself hadn't cost him anything.

Sure, there was a cooktop in the RV. Albert might use it to start a sauce or something. The rest of the time, though, one of the smokers or grills that he'd brought would do all the work.

"You doing okay? Family okay?" Albert asked.

The grin he got in response told him all that he needed to know. "They're all good," Paulo assured him. "Any trouble getting up here?"

"Nope. GPS is a wonder, y'know? And Betty did just fine," Albert assured him.

"Oh, yeah, that's right," Paulo said.

His cheery nature seemed to diminish. The smile he showed to Albert was suddenly forced.

"Hey, we'll win this time. I can feel it, y'know? New place. New start," Albert assured him.

Paulo looked off, over the trees, then nodded. "Yes. New place. It'll be a fresh start."

Then he looked back at Albert, a determined look in his eyes. "Let's get Betty moved over to the competition grounds."

"What, now?" Albert asked, then he shook his head. "Nope. I don't want to take a chance, leaving her all alone at night. We'll stay here tonight, then we'll move her tomorrow morning, first thing."

"We might have to use the RV then, to move her," Paulo said. Turned out that he'd borrowed a truck from his brother that they could use to haul Betty's trailer, as Paulo himself had flown up.

"No, no, that just doesn't feel right," Albert said. "She stays here. Besides, I'm already cooking half-a-dozen pork butts on her, seeing how she does here. We'll be serving customers tastes of that tomorrow, before we start cooking the competition meats."

Paulo looked so disappointed, Albert added, "Let's go over to the competition area, check in, like that."

"All right," Paulo said, though he shook his head and didn't seem pleased with the notion.

The pair of them walked along the paved trail, past other RVs and some of their competitors. Albert didn't recognize many of the names—pit crews that were new to him. Still, he waved at the three women standing around the long offset who had a banner across their RV that read, *Las Chicas de Carne*, as well as the young man with the egg-shaped smoker with a banner proclaiming him *King of Cool Smoke*.

To get to registration, they had to walk through the area set up for the contest. The competitors were arranged in a horseshoe around the edges of a large, cleared field—at least as long as a football field. A stage was being assembled at the open end. Standing next to the stage, to the right, were a couple of long tents, with signs indicating meat turn-in stations.

"This is much bigger than I thought it'd be," Albert admitted as they looked across the open field.

"Think it'll be full of competitors?" Paulo said.

Albert nodded. There were stakes marking out each competitor's area all around the field. "I do," he said. "It also won't matter a lick. We got this."

Paulo nodded. "Yup," he said, though he didn't sound convinced in the least.

That was okay. Albert felt their chances were good.

The people running registration appeared to have a clue about what was going on and how to run a competition (unlike that one event they vowed to never return to, in Kansas). The Smoking Good Q team was assigned a spot in the field, their competition number, when they should set up their offset on the field, and a window during which the meat inspector would come visit them to inspect the meat they'd brought for the contest.

Albert was glad they hadn't brought Betty down. It wasn't that she'd be lonely out on the field all by herself, but it would have made her a target to any mischief makers.

Paulo and Albert went over their strategy for Saturday and Sunday, how they were going to get Betty over to the competition area, the timing of the meats they were cooking, rubs and spices.

Paulo insisted that the judges here weren't brainwashed by the Kansas City Barbecue Association (KCBA), that they didn't need the extreme sweetness preferred by some of the east coast judges.

It was part of why Albert had wanted to try a LCBA contest. He'd read the same things on the online barbecue forums he lurked on.

Now, he wasn't about to go hog wild and give them one of his Chinese five-spice rubs on the pork shoulder.

However, Oregon, or at least Portland, was all about coffee.

Maybe he should use one of his coffee rubs, like on the pork. It had instant espresso powder, thyme, tarragon, smoked paprika, and sage.

Just as they were finishing up their planning, another RV pulled in, right beside them.

Albert couldn't help but grimace. It was a group of idiots that he recognized from some of the KCBA contests that he'd attended. They called themselves HOT Grill Action.

Real competitors might have a shot of whiskey, or even a beer or two, during a contest. Chances were, though, they were completely sober and didn't drink a drop until after they'd turned in all their proteins.

When you had to get up at three or four in the morning to start cooking your brisket, you didn't drink heavily the night before. Or stay up all night. That was for amateurs.

HOT Grill Action was made up of a group of rowdy frat boys, at least as far as Albert was concerned. All twenty some-things who'd just started competition grilling that year. Professional teams had two or three members. These yahoos had twice that, and would only turn in one or two meats.

He would grudgingly admit that they'd had some success. Beginner's luck.

They had no skill, no finesse, and no endurance. He bet

they'd go down hard at a double, when you cooked the same four proteins two nights in a row.

"Wonder when the real competition will arrive," Albert said dryly.

When Paulo didn't reply, Albert glanced over at him.

He'd gone completely pale, as though he'd covered his face in ash for *dia de la muerta*.

"You okay?" Albert asked, tapping his elbow against Paulo's forearm.

Paulo shook his head. "What? Yes." He stared ahead again. "I'm so sorry."

"What the hell you got to be sorry for?" Albert asked. "Those punks ain't gonna beat us."

Paulo visibly gulped. "Yes, yes, you're right. It's going to be fine."

Albert wasn't convinced, and he was damned sure that Paulo wasn't convinced either.

Everything was *not* going to be fine, but Albert had no idea what was wrong, what had spooked Paulo so badly, or how he could fix this.

While still regaining his winning streak.

After Paulo left, Albert stuck to the campsite, never leaving. Even when the idiots across the way started in with their loud rap music.

Gansta rap, despite being as pale as Albert.

As if. They were just a bunch of punks. Would probably piss themselves if they wandered into a real barfight.

Albert felt like a fool going out twice that night to check on

Betty, to make sure that she was still there, still in prime condition.

However, Paulo had gotten Albert spooked.

He felt like less of a fool when the redneck alarm he'd set up—a series of tin cans tied together with a string, attached to one Betty's legs—jangled at three AM.

No one was there by the time Albert made it out the door of the RV.

But he would swear that Betty had been moved. Maybe just an inch to the side of the platform.

Like all good rednecks, Albert kept his granddaddy's old Government Issue Colt in his safe box in the RV.

He wasn't about to pull it out, though, or do something foolish like store it in his boot, unlike that jackass up in Tennessee who blew his own damned foot off.

He reset his redneck alarm, tying the cans to a different leg and making it impossible to move Betty without some sort of noise. Then he tried going back to sleep, but kept waking up every time he heard wind blowing through the trees or the sound of pine needles softly falling on the roof of the RV.

Paulo arrived early, before seven. He was able to borrow his brother's truck again so they could easily transport Betty over to the competition area. Their space was on the lower curve of the horseshoe. If the stage was noon, they were in the five o'clock position.

Albert came prepared with tents, camp chairs, tables, the barrel smoker, and all the cooking and serving gear he needed. Paulo and Albert had set up this sort of stand before, a place where they could meet and talk with customers who came through to try their barbecue. He had the big banners for Smoking Good Q hanging nicely over the tents, along with signs with the QR codes that people could use to get to the food truck's website.

Just that summer, Albert had started selling a few of his rubs. He'd named his line, "Nuthin but Taste" as he'd focused on those recipes that didn't contain nightshades, garlic, or onion. None of them contained gluten, of course, and a bunch were sugar-free as well.

Sure, a few of his competitors thought he'd gone over the bend and was too *foo-foo* to be serving anything good.

Seemed, though, that an awful lot of people wanted to buy those sorts of rubs. Particularly after they tried it at a show.

He'd gotten a food seller's permit for Oregon through the LCBA so he'd brought a wide range of rubs available for people to try, along with the pork butts he'd smoked the day before.

Everything was going to be just fine.

And it was, as the crowds came wandering by, tempted to taste the pork he'd cooked that was melt-in-your-mouth tender. They sold a good number of the jars of rub he'd brought as well.

Albert sent Paulo up back to the RV a few times for forgotten items, though honestly, Albert didn't need them. He just wanted someone going back to the campsite at odd times so that no one would try to do something stupid and sabotage it.

An older, heavy-set woman with salt-and-pepper wild curls came by around two PM. "Hi there. I'm Sally Barker," she said as way of introduction. "Your meat inspector."

Albert shook her hand, impressed by how strong she appeared to be. She'd not spent her life inside, typing on a computer, that was for damned sure, especially based on her ruddy cheeks and weathered skin. She wore a comfortable gray hand-knit cardigan over jeans and heavy boots.

Albert brought her back to the rear of his setup and showed her the coolers where he'd kept the competition meat. Sally professionally examined every piece, making sure that it was being kept at a safe temperature, was still in the original packaging, and that nothing had been added to it, like some sort of marinade.

Sally chatted easily as she went about her business, asking about where they'd come from, how long they'd been doing competitions, the different types of smokers they'd be using.

It wasn't until after the inspection was over and she'd handed them their certificate that she asked about the rubs. She appeared impressed that Albert had the "Nuthin but Taste" line.

"Got a niece who I swear is allergic to just about everything but water," she commented as Albert explained the basic rub that was free of the eight most common allergen.

"I hear you," Albert commented. "Have a step-daughter who's the same way, who inspired most of this line."

Sally put down the rub with a sigh. "I need to finish my rounds, first. But I'm coming back for that."

"I'll put aside a jar for you," Albert told her. He knew he couldn't just offer it to her, as that might be seen as a bribe.

Everything had to be on the up-and-up. Particularly as he was planning on replacing his losing streak with a winning one.

Late in the afternoon, he made the decision that he'd stay down in the competition area, with Betty, all night. He made Paulo bring down a cot and a sleeping bag and they rearranged the cooking schedule, so that Albert could take care of the meat.

Pork butts were going on first, as he tended to cook his for sixteen hours. Next, the brisket would go on at three AM, as it also needed a lot of time to cook. After that came the ribs, then the chicken last. The judging would be blind, meaning the judges would have no idea who turned in what box.

The contest turn-in times for when the meats had to be ready for the judges were varied. Chicken at noon on Sunday, ribs at twelve-thirty, brisket at one, and pork at one-thirty. Turn-in times were tightly controlled, and a contestant only had a ten-minute window to get their boxes turned in.

It would mean a lot of work in the middle of the day, as Albert tried to schedule everything exactly, getting the boxes set up and delivering those at the perfect time, so the meat would still be warm and appetizing for the judges.

Then, Albert could relax a little. While he was busy with the cooking, Paulo would be handling the crowds coming through, talking with customers, handing out samples, selling rubs.

If Albert could have afforded it, he'd have three people, like *Las Chicas de Carnes* who were just a couple of stands away from him, closer to the six o'clock location. That way, he could have two people prepping boxes while the third handled everything else.

However, Oregon was a long-ass haul from Texas, and he didn't expect anyone to come along for free.

As his dad had drilled into his head, if your business model depends on slave wages, it ain't much of a business model. The only way Albert had been able to afford this trip was because Paolo had volunteered to go to Oregon on his own.

Hopefully, they'd sell enough rubs and place high enough in the various categories that Albert would show a profit. Competitions were mainly for the prestige, advertising, and the sponsorships. As he was based in Texas, he wouldn't see a bump in his food truck business by coming all the way out here.

However, maybe the online store would.

The day drew to a close and the crowds of customers dwindled. Albert had already put the pork butts on Betty, at the far end of the offset, so they'd cook low and slow all night.

The firebox was heavily insulated so once it got hot, it stayed hot. However, the smoker itself wasn't insulated. As the temperature dropped, Albert put Betty's coat on her—a bright red thermal blanket that had been tailored to fit the offset perfectly. This would keep the temperature more even along the long barrel, and he'd need less fuel.

For this cook, he was starting with mesquite wood, as that was plentiful and cheap in Texas, but would be an exotic flavor up here in Oregon. It added a lovely, sweeter smoke, which would be perfect for the pork. Later on, when he put the brisket into Betty, he would start adding more hickory to the firebox, to give the smoke a more robust flavor, appropriate for beef.

He'd cook both the ribs and the chicken on the barrel smoker. For this contest, he'd use natural charcoal instead of wood, as both meats would have sauces. All that he needed to develop taste-wise was a kiss of smoke. The flavor of the smoke would be less important.

Finally, Albert sent Paulo back to his family, not allowing the other man to stick around, even though they'd originally set up the schedule with Paulo doing the first shift and Albert doing the second.

No, Albert needed to spend the night tending to Betty. Particularly after the redneck alarm had gone off the night before.

Paulo had questioned whether or not the wind had just blown the tin cans over.

Albert was convinced, though, that Betty had been moved.

At least staying here, at the event space, meant he wasn't subjected to that stupid rap that the HOT Grill Action team was playing. They had played it for a short while until one of the women from *Las Chicas de Carne* went over and talked with them. She reported back that their player had gotten too hot and burned out, or something like that.

Albert spent some time that evening hanging out with *Las Chicas*, Gabby, Cecilia, and Elenore. Nice women, totally into barbecue. They had a food truck down in San Francisco and had done more than one LCBA event. They'd assured him that what he'd heard was correct—the LCBA judges didn't need the sweetness that the KCBA judges preferred.

When he got back to his camp, he did an inspection of everything, Betty, the barrel smoker, all his equipment.

It all seemed to be just fine.

He arranged the redneck alarm again, set his alarm for an hour ahead of when he actually needed to get up to put on the brisket, and went to sleep quickly, given the night before hadn't been great, his dreams filled with sweet smoke and sweeter victory.

Albert awoke with a start, before the alarm went off.

Someone was there, at the site, with him.

He quietly slipped out of his sleeping bag, snagging his flashlight but not turning it on, then walked toward the figure standing at the back of Betty.

A ripping sound filled the quiet night.

Albert flipped on his light.

Paulo stood there with a knife in hand.

"What are you doing?" Albert asked quietly.

He'd had his suspicions. Some of the bad luck he'd been having had been just that.

However, too many time it had seemed as though someone was out to get him.

Sometimes, it isn't just paranoia.

Paulo stood frozen, his face pale in the harsh light.

"I'm sorry, boss," he said softly. "I didn't want to."

Albert nodded. "Someone is making you."

Paulo stood silent, still frozen.

"Blackmail?" Albert guessed. It was the only thing he could think of that would turn one of his crew against him.

Finally, Paulo moved, giving Albert a sharp nod.

Albert took a deep breath, letting it out in a white fog cloud.

"Come on," he said quietly. "Let's make some coffee. Then you can tell me all about it."

Paulo shook his head. "I can't."

"Yes, you can," Albert said. "You don't want to betray me, or the crew. I know that. Otherwise, you would have been more efficient at stopping me. What did you do this time, by the way?"

"Sliced through Betty's coat," Paulo said. "So the temperature wouldn't stay up."

"I'm going to come over and see the damage," Albert said softly. "Then we're having coffee together. Understand me?"

Though Paulo still looked as though he wanted to bolt, he stayed where he was.

At least Albert had gotten there quick enough that only a

single slash marred the back of Betty's coat. Some duck-tape would hold that together just fine.

After doing a quick repair, Albert made them some coffee, then put out two chairs.

Paulo still looked as though he wanted to run. But he stayed, slumping down into the chair, looking like a dog afraid that he was about to be beaten. Again.

"I didn't want to betray you," Paulo said after the coffee had warmed them both up a touch.

"I know that," Albert said. "That's why I only had my flashlight and not my gun."

Paulo gave him a watery smile. "See? You're so much smarter than I am."

Albert snorted at that. He was a redneck, and could figure stuff out sometimes. Not smart at all.

Just look at his past with Rebecca and others.

As deep as a mud-puddle, she'd said once.

Paulo seemed stuck, still trying to find the words, so Albert asked, "Is it the HOT Grill Action crew? Do they have something on you?"

Paulo shivered. "Yeah. They do."

"What?" Albert asked, possibly a bit sharply. His patience was only going to last so long. "Tell me so that we can fix this."

"You aren't going to want to help me after I tell you," Paulo warned.

"Let me be the judge of that," Albert said.

Paulo looked off across the dark field for a few moments, gathering together his courage, before he finally said all in a rush, "I'm gay."

Albert waited for a moment, waiting for the other shoe. Finally, he said, "So?"

Paulo wrenched his head back and stared hard at Albert. "What do you mean, 'so'?"

Albert shrugged. "You do know my older brother's gay, right?"

Paulo looked shocked. "No! I thought he was married!"

"He was," Albert said, nodding. "Absolute witch of a woman. Probably married her as some sort of punishment for himself. Finally divorced her and admitted his true nature. He still has awful tastes in partners though." Albert paused, thinking for a few moments. "You dating anyone?"

Paulo snorted. "No."

"Remind me to introduce you to Ellis at some point," Albert said, nodding.

Paulo blinked, still in shock. "That's it? You don't care?"

"I may look like a redneck who'd be comfortable wearing sheets and singing to Hitler, but I'm a grown adult and able to make my decisions," Albert said firmly.

"Wow," Paulo said, shaking head. He obviously hadn't been expecting this reaction at all.

"I honestly don't care who you're sleeping with. As long as it's all consenting adults, I'm fine." Albert paused, then added, "No, aslong as it isn't a vegetarian. Or god forbid, a vegan."

Paulo finally started laughing at that. A little hysterically to start with, for sure, but the laughter faded and he ended with a true smile on his face. "You truly don't care."

"That's right. I don't. So what does the HOT Grill Action team have on you? A video? Pictures?"

"Something like that, yeah," Paulo said. "They recorded me in the men's restroom in Georgia."

"All right, so first off, act like an adult and get a room next time, okay?" Albert said.

Paulo nodded, abashed. "My family didn't know, either,"

he said softly. "It's why I came up. They were mostly like you, though my *abela* said she'd always known and that it was about time I came out."

"Grandmothers know everything," Albert said. His own had been a scary woman who he'd sworn more than once had had the ability to read minds, though she claimed it was just auras she saw.

"What type of device did they record you on?" Albert asked after a few moments.

"Camera," Paulo admitted. "It was kind of weird. Like they were all prepared or something."

"Uhm, was that restroom something of a pickup spot?" Albert said, not sure if he wanted to hear the answer or not.

"It is!" Paulo said enthusiastically. "See, the end stall is just the right size—"

"Spare me the details." Albert sat for a few moments, drumming his fingers on the arm of his chair. "Every accusation is a confession, or so I've been told. Do you think there's any chance that when they went in there, they'd been planning on taking advantage of the, uhm, accommodations, themselves?"

"Maybe," Paulo said. "I wasn't really paying attention to them."

"Do you think you could persuade one of them into a dalliance? So that I could come in and record it?" While Albert didn't really want to see such an act, he also really couldn't think of any way else of getting Paulo out from under this thing.

Until Paulo came out to everyone, and decided that he just didn't care anymore.

He shook his head. "That's a good way of getting my ass

kicked." Then he paused. "But maybe, if I just went to talk with Erik, alone..."

"You think on that," Albert said. "I'll see if I can figure out some other way to get some dirt on them."

Paulo jumped up out of his chair. "I'm going to go take a better look at the restrooms here. See if there's a good place for a hookup."

"All right," Albert said. He glanced at his watch. "May as well start the fire in Betty, get her ready for the brisket."

The fire caught nicely—no problems starting her at all. Had Paulo been responsible for that one time when she wouldn't light and stay lit? Possibly.

Albert was concerned when Paulo didn't come back right away.

Surely he wasn't stupid enough to "try out" those "accommodations" tonight, was he?

Finally, Paulo came bursting back into the camp.

"You'll never guess who I found already 'using' the restroom!" he exclaimed, explaining how he'd found two of the HOT Grill Action team in "action" and had recorded them on his phone before they'd realized he was there.

"Good!" Albert said. He was happy he hadn't had to go and do that part himself. "So, tomorrow, you, me, and maybe Gabby from *Las Chicas* need to go and confront those idiots."

Paulo blinked in surprise. "Why bring in an outsider?"

Albert just grinned at him. "While Gabby and Cecelia are sisters, Elanore is Gabby's girlfriend."

"Oh. Oh!" Paulo said. He paused for a moment. "You really aren't bothered by this."

"When I was young and stupid, I might have been," Albert admitted. "But hopefully, we all grow up at some point and realize that it's absolutely none of our business."

Paulo nodded and eventually left, Albert still tending the fires while Paulo went up to the RV to sleep. Tomorrow would be another busy day, and they both needed to be at their best.

Albert hoped that without the sabotage, he really would regain his winning streak.

Meeting with the HOT Grill Action team had gone better than Albert could have hoped. The members of the team started accusing each other of all sorts of lewd behavior, shouting and shoving each other around, like the rowdy frat boys they were.

They didn't end up disqualifying themselves, though it was touch and go for a while, particularly after the contest officials got involved due to the prolonged shouting match going on.

However, they didn't place high in the ranks at all, much to Albert's satisfaction. He hoped it would be the last he saw of them for quite a while.

*Las Chicas* placed well, taking first in ribs, seventh in brisket, tenth in pork, and way down in the bottom for chicken.

Gabby and Albert commiserated, as he hadn't even reached the top ten in chicken either.

It was just such a hard protein to get right!

However, the rest of the Smoking Good Q scores were right in line with where they should be: fifth in ribs, third in brisket, and second in pork.

The team who scored the highest in all four categories was awarded the Grand Champion trophy for the entire competition. Though Albert had snagged more than one of those in previous contests, he only made third overall this time.

Still, not bad for an inaugural run of a competition, as well as his first time with the LCBA.

As Albert drove away from Oregon on Monday morning, Paulo quietly riding in the passenger seat, Albert reflected again on how he loved barbecue competition.

Going to them, competing in them, and then, winning them.

Lili sat at her campsite, alone as usual, watching over her smokers and her various meat as it cooked. All around her, other contestants who in the Wide River BBQ competition tended to their own cooks. Like Lili, they'd gotten up around three AM to start their brisket, to give it time to cook and then rest before turning it into the judges at one PM. It was too early yet for the smell of cooking beef to overtake the scent of burning wood and charcoal. In a couple of hours though, the scent would be so thick Lili would feel like she needed another shower to clean it off her skin.

At least this campground had trees between the sites. Lili hated it when she was sandwiched between two huge RVs, like they were camping together in a huge parking lot. It meant seeing people all the time, having to remember to be polite, to smile. Even to make small talk, which was the worst.

To be honest, though, being so packed in wasn't all bad. It meant she could hear the laughter of her neighbors in their RVs. Maybe get a sample of their "special sauce" that they refused to list out the ingredients for. Listening to the other teams complain about the current contest (or the weather) always made her want to speak up and say, "Me too!"

However, it was also a reminder that she went from one barbecue contest to the next by herself. Everyone else had a team, or at least a partner they could rely on.

Lili was alone. And while sometimes she preferred that, every so often, she felt lonely.

That was why she'd created a profile on an online dating app that was just for barbecue enthusiasts, appropriately named "Meat Lovers." Of course, there were a few crude applicantes and many innuendos about the name.

Lili had found some kindred spirits though.

Before she swiped over to the app on her tablet, she double-checked her smoker. TechGril, the company sponsoring her at the barbecue competitions that summer, was having her test one of their newest product lines.

First, Lili checked the software running the fans and thermometers, making sure they were working as expected. She did a dump of the logs and checked for errors or inconsistencies. Then she physically checked the smoker itself, using three different probes, verifying that the digital readouts matched the physical ones.

The smoker looked like an upright oil barrel, about two feet across and three feet tall, painted black with TechGrill's nerdy-green logo done in a stripe running at a slant up the back of it. The front had several doors for accessing the different parts of the smoker, and the silver domed top came off as well.

So far, the company's smoker had been working as perfectly as the smokers Lili had customized herself. She'd found the charcoal pan at the bottom easy to refill. The water pan, which was located right above the bed of coals, only needed refilling every eight hours or so, even when running at a high temperature. The fans and the thermometers regulated the temperature accurately—only a three degree difference between the top and the bottom of the smoker, which was well within even Lili's exacting tolerance.

That was part of Lili's problem, though. The new smokers were working too well. This meant that there was little for Lili to do. She'd prepped her pork shoulder and set it to cook before she'd gone to bed and gotten a little sleep on the cot in her tent. Now, the brisket was cooking. She had an alarm set and would spray the brisket with her special sauce every hour. (And no, she wouldn't share what exactly was in it either.) She wouldn't have a lot to do until she started the ribs at five. They required spritzing every fifteen minutes for the first three hours of their cook.

After the ribs were on, she had to prep the chicken thighs. Just thinking about that made her despair. Getting chicken right felt nearly impossible. Making the proportions identical and getting the cook even was challenging enough. The few times she'd felt confident that she'd achieved that, there was still something off in her flavor profile. She'd yet to win any prizes for her chicken, let alone place high in any competition.

There was nothing demanding her attention right now. The water in the pans was full, and she didn't need to add more charcoal for a while.

She could try to sleep for the next forty-two minutes, until she had to spritz the brisket.

Or she could go onto Meat Lovers and see if she could find someone to chat with.

Of course, she had two-factor authentication set up on her profile when she signed in. Who wouldn't? So it took her a few extra minutes to sign in, as she had to retrieve her phone to get the code. That security was well worth her peace of mind. At least the site itself was vaguely secure, and didn't have too many third party calls.

She would have coded it up differently, but she was no longer a software developer these days. Not really. The small bit of coding that she'd done on her original smokers, and the fans and thermometers that she ran with a Raspberry PI, didn't really count. Nor did checking the logs on the new grills.

As soon as she signed in, Jason pinged her. It made her glad, as he was one of her favorite people to chat with.

If she was being honest, he was the only one she chatted with regularly. Mostly she told people, "No thank you" and blocked them when they tried to suggest something inappropriate.

Of course, she knew that Jason wasn't this person's real name. Why would anyone use their real name on an app like this? She used the name "Cha Ming," which kind of sounded like *charming*, and the absolute opposite of her own personality. It was a hint to her Asian heritage, though. Her parents had come over from Korea, but Lili considered herself American. She was tall—almost five foot eleven—with a thin, athletic build, scraggly black hair that she always wore pulled back, a flat face and Asian features.

For her avatar, Lili used the image of a cartoon robot wearing an apron. It was in the appropriate colors, peach and black, which was what she wore every day. (Having an entire wardrobe made up of the same colors meant one less decision she had to make in the mornings.)

Jason used an image of a Greek sailing ship for his avatar, for Jason and the Argonauts.

He'd been asking Lili about her real name. And also for her to send him a picture.

So far, Lili had resisted. She didn't want another photo of her out on the internet. There had been enough of those, what with her being accused of killing someone last spring. Luckily, AJ and Gabby had been able to help clear her name.

*Hey there. Figured you'd be signing on sometime soon. You're at a contest this weekend, right?*

Lili hadn't told Jason where she'd be, but she wasn't surprised. It felt nice that someone checked in on her regularly and followed her schedule. Not stalkerish.

*Yes. Cooking. Just put brisket on. Pork's
been on since last night. Got a good
feeling about it. Trying a new recipe
for the rub.*

Jason came back a few minutes later. Lili always wondered if the lag was because of app itself or if Jason's connection just wasn't that good.

*More fennel in the rub this time, right?
Should give it a nice sweet flavor.*

*Yes. And smoked coriander seeds, with
paprika and garlic.*

*Can't go wrong with garlic.*

*What are you doing up at this time?*

Lili waited for the reply to come back. Jason had admitted to being on the west coast, like Lili. While there were a lot of barbecue competitions down south and on the east coast, Lili preferred the Left Coast BBQ Association (LCBA) rules to those of the Kansas City BBQ Association (KCBA). They allowed her to experiment more. In addition, LCBA judges were more open to different flavors than the KCBA judges.

Plus, there were a lot of specialty LCBA contests, ones that only did two of the traditional four proteins (pulled pork, brisket, ribs, chicken) plus something else, like salmon, top round, or ribeye. She'd be going to one of those next weekend.

Jason finally messaged her back and told her that he couldn't sleep that night. Lili nodded in sympathy, though he couldn't see her. He'd told her about his night terrors, waking up horribly disoriented and unable to go back to sleep. Lili wasn't sure what in his past had caused such things—he hadn't gone into more details and she hadn't asked. Still, she was glad that she could be there for him when he needed to chat with someone.

So they talked about the upcoming contest, who Lili thought would be her stiffest competition that weekend, how her own cook was going.

As they were winding up their conversation—Lili had just put the ribs on and had to start prepping chicken—Jason made his usual request.

*Sure would love to see a pic sometime...*

Lili looked around her campsite. The sun was already rising and she could see things much more clearly. Her tablet took pictures without any identifiable information. She'd written her own filters to make sure of it, scrubbing any photos clean. So she took a picture of her campsite, the three smokers steaming in the cool air. It was nicely atmospheric, if she did say so herself. She scrutinized the pic for a few moments, making sure that there wasn't anything readily identifiable in the shot, then she sent it to him via the app.

*Nice pic! Here's something for you as well.*

Lili scrunched up her face when she was the photo that came through. It was of a young white man, with black hair that had the ends dyed blond. Incredibly handsome, with a perfectly proportioned nose and a cleft chin. A white ring reflected off his brown eyes, the sort of lighting used in a professional shoot.

*Is that supposed to be you?*

Lili downloaded the picture, then fretted while Jason took a more time than usual to reply.

*Of course! Why would I send a picture*
*of a stranger to you? Won't you*
*please send me one back?*

Lili signed off the app instead of answering.

She didn't have time to check right now. She had ribs to spritz and chicken thighs to prep. A contest to possibly win, or at least place in.

However, despite his assurances, she would bet that the picture that Jason had just sent wasn't him.

Before Lili could do an internet search on the photo that Jason had sent her, Gabby walked into her campsite. Even though Gabby was a competitor—she was the fire mistress of Las Chicas de Carne—she was still a friend. Albeit a bit scary.

The other woman was very short and very round, with long black hair and Hispanic features. Lili's mother wouldn't have approved of Gabby's weight and would have made many snide comments about it in Korean.

There was a chance, though, that even Lili's mother wouldn't have said much about her friend's appearance. Particularly not if Gabby gave her *that look*, the one that felt like a volcano was about to explode in your face and there was nothing you could do to protect yourself from the oncoming lava flow.

"We're having some breakfast," Gabby said without preamble. "Smoked breakfast burritos."

It warmed Lili all the way through that Gabby understood just how little Lili wanted to make small talk, so she never started with asking how Lili was, how she'd slept, or even how her cook was going. In addition, food made by Las Chicas wasn't something even Lili would turn down lightly. She checked her timer.

"Four minutes, twenty-three seconds," Lili said.

Gabby nodded, understanding that was how long Lili had before she had to do something with her proteins and was free to leave her camp for a while.

"How's your schedule?" Gabby asked, having learned that Lili never wanted to talk about how she was doing, never knew how to answer such a question.

"On time for everything," Lili said. She didn't have to force a smile, either, or try to sound more animated, which always left her exhausted. No, Gabby, Gabby's sister Cecelia, and Gabby's girlfriend, Elanor, all understood about Lili's very limited social abilities.

Just as Jason had.

"Why the sour face?" Gabby asked.

Lili was surprised that she had reacted so strongly to thinking about Jason that Gabby could see it.

"Jason," Lili said.

Gabby knew who Lili was talking about. "What did he do?"

"Sent me a photo that he claimed was him, but I think it's fake," Lili said.

"Do you know for certain?" Gabby said.

"Not yet. Don't want to know yet," Lili admitted. She wanted to hold out the hope that Jason hadn't lied to her so badly, destroying their friendship.

"Come on over to camp. Don't check on the picture until later," Gabby advised. "After turn in."

Lili nodded. That made sense, actually. She needed to focus on her cook, on her putting the best product she could in front of the judges. After she'd turned in all four of her meats, then she could worry about Jason.

"Agreed," Lili said.

That took some of the pressure off her. She spritzed her ribs, then followed Gabby back to the campsite of Las Chicas, effectively putting Jason out of her mind.

For now.

Lili walked along side Gabby back to her campsite after turning in her last protein, the pulled pork. The contest rules only required pulled pork, not the pieces that were called burnt ends —the crispy edges of the meat that, when done right, were tangy, crunchy, smoky, yet still tasted like pork. She'd felt confident enough in her cook that she'd included both the pulled pork as well as the burnt ends in her box.

That wasn't what was causing butterflies in her stomach, though. No, she was going to have to go searching for that photo, to verify that Jason had sent her a false photo.

If he'd just admitted to it being a fake, she would have been okay. Then she could have sent him a false picture and felt good about it.

Claiming that it was real had left her very unsettled.

Everyone knew that no one used their real names or real pictures online. At least, no one with a lick of sense. Jason had always seemed so much smarter than to claim a false photo as his own.

"So let's do this," Gabby said as they reached Lili's site.

Lili sighed and brought her tablet out of the locked safe in the back of her truck. Gabby politely didn't crowd Lili as she signed in, but did come over and sit down on the park-provided picnic table when Lili beckoned her over. (Of course, Lili had cleaned the rough wood thoroughly, three times, before putting down the washable tablecloth and seat covers.)

"That's the picture Jason sent?" Gabby asked when Lili pulled it up.

Lili just nodded, still miserable.

"Why do you think it's fake?"

"Someone who looks like that wouldn't be interested in someone like me," Lili said straight off.

Before Gabby could object, Lili continued. "That picture was also professionally taken. See the ring of lights reflected in his eyes? Regular people don't have or use lights like that. Plus, see the contours of his cheeks? The picture's been run through some sort of filter. Probably more than one."

"All right," Gabby said slowly. "So what do you do now?"

Lili opened up a website used to search on images, then dragged and dropped the photo onto the search box.

She didn't have to hold her breath for long.

Not only was the image not of Jason, it was from a stock photo site, part of some model shoot.

"Any chance that Jason's actually a model?" Gabby asked.

"No. He's a software developer. Like I was," Lili said. "And I know that's true because we've been able to talk coding at a pretty deep level. That isn't something someone can fake."

She frowned. Or at least she didn't think someone could fake that sort of knowledge. Particularly Python, the language she'd used to program her Raspberry Pi. Or the running argument they had about the virtues of using C++ instead.

"It appears that photo is used in a lot of places," Gabby said, reading over Lili's shoulder.

There were a few social media profiles that all used that same picture. Or other pictures from this photoshoot.

And more than one of those profiles belonged to a Jason, someone called The Argonaut, as well as just JA.

Including a site that took cash electronically.

"Has Jason ever asked for money from you?" Gabby asked.

"No," Lili said. She felt crushed, as if the program she'd been working on for months had suddenly been wiped out and all her backups had turned out to be corrupt.

"What do I do?" Lili said, her voice as broken as her heart. She wasn't certain of anything, now. Had Jason been lying to her about everything this entire time? Did he have night terrors? Was he even a real person, or someone's AI? She'd been accused of being a robot her entire life. Maybe she'd been fooled by one.

"Do you care for this Jason?" Gabby said. "Really care?"

Lili took a deep breath and let it out. She wasn't normally too physical, or tied to her body. However, even she could tell that tension had taken over.

"Yeah, I do," Lili said. He'd been the only one there for her at her darkest times. She'd never told him about being accused of killing someone, as that would have made her too identifiable. She'd just told him that she'd been in trouble. And he'd been there for her, at all hours, while she'd been going through that. "And I think he cares about me to," she added, her voice a mere whisper.

"Then you confront him," Gabby said. "Tell him you know the picture is a fake. That you believe he has other social media accounts."

"It's called catfishing, what he's doing," Lili said. "Pretending to be someone else."

"Do you want me to stay here while you chat with him?" Gabby asked.

After a few moments of consideration, Lili finally replied, "No."

"Come over to our site afterwards, when you're ready," Gabby told Lili in a tone that even Lili, and her poor ability to read people, knew was on the scary side and brooked no argument.

"I will," Lili promised, glad that she hadn't been given a timeline, that she could just do this as she needed to.

She didn't want to confront Jason. Non-confrontational had been her style her entire life.

But she owed this to herself to get to the bottom of who this person actually was.

She'd faced down a killer, after all.

She could face down a catfisher.

Jason's first message, as soon as he saw Lili online, was

*How'd the turn in go?*

Lili stared at the message for a few moments before replying.

*I know that photo wasn't yours. It's from*

> *a stock photo site. And it's associated*
> *with a bunch of profiles that look*
> *like they belong to you.*

She paused, her heart pounding, before she hit enter, sending the message along.

That he replied so quickly surprised her.

> *I know, I'm sorry, that was stupid to*
> *send you that picture. You know how*
> *to look those things up.*

Lili thought for a moment before replying.

> *That implies that you have sent that*
> *picture before, to other people. Just*
> *how many profiles do you have? How*
> *many people are you talking with?*
> *Are you a catfisher? Are you taking*
> *money from people?*

In retrospect, Lili realized that she shouldn't have been surprised when Jason suddenly went offline.

So, that was it. She no longer had Jason in her life. What little friendship and companionship that she'd had was now gone.

She was all alone.

As usual.

Lili briefly debated deleting her profile on Meat Lovers, but decided that was just one thing too many. Instead, she headed dutifully down to see Las Chicas, to wait for the judges results with them.

Gabby didn't ask how she was, but instead, directed Lili to helping her clean out Inez, their big offset smoker. The grill grates were particularly sticky—Elanor had been experimenting with a new sauce—and Lili was grateful for the work, applying her skills at cleaning to a new problem.

Eventually, they all headed over to the judging area. It surprised Lili that she actually managed to get to seventh place in chicken, the highest she'd ever scored. She didn't do well in the brisket, which she expected, or the ribs. But she managed third place with her pulled pork.

Despite how everyone congratulated her, Lili's victory felt hollow to her.

She found herself reaching for her phone, to send a quick note to Jason about how well she'd done.

But there was no Jason.

She still dutifully entered all the teams' ranks into her spreadsheet, keep track of how everyone else did.

Las Chicas scored second in ribs as well as pork, though they'd also had issues with their brisket and ribs. It appeared that Elanor's new sauce had been a hit, and she was already talking about how to modify it for the other proteins.

Jack Jackson scored well enough in all the categories to be ranked the Grand Champion of the entire competition. He generally did win, though, so Lili wasn't that angry at him.

She enjoyed a celebration meal with Las Chicas before heading back to her camp.

Alone.

Again.

As usual.

Out of habit, she still pulled up the Meat Lovers app. She hadn't deleted her profile, after all.

She saw that she had a message waiting from Jason.

Should she read it? She didn't want to. But she couldn't just delete it unread, though.

"Hey there," she suddenly heard. "You okay?"

Lili looked up. Gabby was standing just outside the light from her campfire. She seemed to catch the glow of the fire and throw it back.

"He left me a message," Lili said.

"Do you want me to read it for you?" Gabby asked gently, stepping forward, taking on a more regular appearance.

Though she still looked fierce. Lili was glad to be on the right side with her.

"Sure," Lili said, handing her tablet to Gabby.

"Huh," was not what she expected Gabby to say.

"What is it?"

"He says that yes, he is a catfisher, that he's sorry, and that he's been trying to quit. He, uhm, knows you don't have to forgive him, knows that you don't owe him anything, but he'd like your help quitting all the lies," Gabby said.

"Do you believe him?" Lili said.

Gabby shrugged. "I don't know him," she said. "But I have a feeling that he's sincere. That he does want to quit."

"I don't want to help him," Lili said. She was still reeling and hurt from finding out that Jason wasn't really the person she thought he was, that he did this with lots of other people.

That she wasn't special.

Had that been why there had always been a delay when she'd been chatting with him? Had he been chatting with other people at the same time as well?

"We helped you when no one else was around," Gabby pointed out.

"I was innocent," Lili said stubbornly.

"True," Gabby said as she handed the tablet back to Lili.

"I'd still think about it, and not dismiss his call for help out of hand."

"Why?" Lili asked. She didn't owe Jason anything, despite how he'd helped her and always been there for her.

Did she?

"I have a good feeling about this," was all that Gabby said. "I think that, in the end, you'll be able to help each other."

With that, Gabby turned and walked away, the fire still outlining her even after she'd passed out of range.

Lili shook her head, and the full darkness came back.

She must be imagining things. Or she was more tired than she'd realized.

She read the note that Jason had sent, mulling over the possibilities.

Though Jason had helped her, he'd also lied to her. She scrolled back through their conversations and yes, he'd told her that she was the only one he was chatting to. Maybe he'd just meant on the Meat Lovers app.

Or maybe he'd been lying to her then, too.

Lili knew that she'd never be able to sleep, despite her ability to compartmentalize. This was too big.

Emotions were just too much of a logistical nightmare.

So she sent him a brief message back, that she'd be willing to help him and they'd talk in the morning.

Then she signed off and went to lay down and think for the rest of the night.

It didn't surprise Lili that Jason had kept detailed records about everyone he chatted with. He had the same sort of analytical mind that she did.

He'd never found anything to focus his attention on, though. Or that gave him what he needed, emotionally.

It did surprise her how open Jason was about everything he'd been doing. It seemed that he really was trying to quit.

At Gabby's suggestion, Lili had Jason send a farewell text to all the people he'd been chatting with, explaining that he had some personal issues that he needed to deal with and that he was going offline for a while. It was just polite for him to do that, and to not leave all those people hanging, always wondering where their friend Jason had gone.

Jason gave her full access to his entire online existence: passwords, profiles, everything. Turned out that his real name was Theodore, a name he despised. Along with Theo, Teddy, and Ted. Jason was just a name that he'd chosen for himself, and while it wasn't what was on his birth certificate, it had always felt more like him.

Only after Lili learned Jason's full identity (that she verified, of course) did she offer her own real name. They eventually exchanged phone numbers, and were constantly texting. No phone calls—neither of them were that good "in person" as it were.

Jason admitted to needing the attention he got. He went into therapy, learning that he was trying to make up for a perceived lack in himself, how a lot of it came from shame, of never being able to perform up to his parents' standards.

Lili found herself opening up, growing more, dealing with some of her own demons.

Turned out, the pair of them actually really did love barbecue, it wasn't something that Jason had made up as an interest to chat with her. They both nerded out on different meats, rubs, and cook times, even if all he had was a far inferior pellet grill. Plus, Jason *was* a developer, and worked part-time from home, doing contract jobs instead of a full-time gig for a single corporation. It meant he had a lot of free time, more so than most people.

After three months of intensive chatting—sometimes at all hours of the night, even when Lili wasn't doing a competition cook—they finally agreed to meet. Lili's competition that weekend had just ended, and though she'd told Jason where she was headed next, she could always change her plans in case the meeting in person didn't go well.

Or if it well really well, and she wanted to spend more time with someone in person.

Gabby went with her to the small town that was just outside of the campground where they'd stayed for the competition. They'd found a cute 1950s style diner that supposedly served real barbecue, though both Gabby and Lili had their doubts.

Lili wore her usual peach colored T-shirt and black jeans. She knew she looked good in them, though she figured Jason wasn't someone who would worry too much about her looks.

Gabby was in a bright pink-and-black striped shirt with stretch navy-blue jeans. Her own black hair was done in a fat braid down her back, with flowers woven in. She'd offered to do a French braid on Lili's hair, but though touched, Lili had declined.

She'd wanted Jason to see her just as she was, split-ends and all.

As they walked up to the restaurant, Lili saw a youngish man waiting out front. He had a head full of sandy blond curls that looked barely restrained, blue eyes, wearing a nice short-sleeved shirt that was white with thin red stripes and clean blue jeans.

He gave her a smile that lit up his entire face, like the way some customers did when they tasted Lili's pork.

"Jason?" Lili asked as they drew up close.

It was only then that she noticed that he barely came up to her shoulder. He was an inch or so taller than Gabby's five foot two, but just barely.

"Yes," he said. "Lili?"

She nodded at him, trying to give him a smile as she knew was expected of her.

She was so bad in person.

"And this is Gabby," Lili said, introducing her friend.

"Thank you for helping," Jason said seriously.

Gabby peered at him intently.

"Do the right thing," she said ominously. "Or else."

Jason gulped.

Lili found her smile growing more natural.

Gabby really could be downright scary sometimes.

The three of them went into the diner and seated themselves in one of the red vinyl booths, ordering barbecue, a milkshake (for Jason) and Italian sodas made with coconut milk (for Gabby and Lili, who couldn't tolerate dairy too well).

Lili found herself just listening as Jason and Gabby chatted about the most recent barbecue contest, which Lili had won third place this time for chicken. Again.

It wasn't until they were all talking about meat and rubs that she could contribute more, getting more involved in the conversation.

After the meal was finished (and they'd all decided that while the barbecue in the diner was adequate, it was also pedestrian) that Lili found herself running out of words again.

Her phone beeped—a text message.

*I'm really glad to see you. It fills my
heart with joy.*

Lili looked up, a smile naturally forming. Seemed that
Jason had pre-programmed a text, just for her.

He understood that sometimes, she would be tongue-tied.
And he wanted her to know that he still cared for her.

*Ditto*

Was all that Lili wrote back, but she saw his eyes light up
when he read the message.

Gabby left the pair of them soon after that, and silence
descended on the booth.

Jason deliberately pulled up his phone and texted Lili.

*What would you like to do now?*

Lili nodded when she received the message. It was easier to
text him. She was glad he'd thought of that.

*Would you like to come and see my
campsite? My far superior grills?*

Jason gave her a quick grin when he read that.

"I'd like that," he said.

"I was actually hoping you'd come for dinner," Lili said.

Jason nodded, growing more serious as he thought for a
few moments, before he texted her.

*I took this next week off from work. If*

> *you think you might need help with*
> *the next BBQ contest...*

Lili felt her heart grow still, the world put on pause as she considered.

She'd been hoping to find someone who would be a partner in her barbecue business. Someone who understood her, and who loved the world of smoked meat as much as she did.

While she and Jason may have had something of a rocky patch, she had grown to trust him as well as to depend on him always being there.

To have him present in body as well as in spirit might be the best thing to have happened to her.

Finally, Lili nodded. But instead of voicing her assent, she texted him back.

> *Yes, I would like the company. As long as*
> *you have your own tent and*
> *camping space.*

She looked up. Jason nodded.

> *Good. Then let's get back to my site. I*
> *have a meal to prep. Dinner. For the*
> *two of us.*

Jason just grinned.

> *Whatcha cooking?*

> *Catfish.*

# Recipes

What sort of cozy mystery about barbecue would this be without recipes?

I, the author, am allergic to nightshades. This means no chiles, no tomatoes, no potatoes or eggplant.

This is partially why Albert and the "Nuthin' but Taste" line of products exists. Just imagine that every recipe you see from me actually comes from his line.

While I could do some of these under the Las Chicas' banner, they're much more known for their spice, and if I add chilies, I can't taste it.

So here are a couple of my favorite recipes. Enjoy!

## CCP RUB

This rub does have a surprising level of heat to it. That's from the amount of black pepper that I add. In addition, I generally add a little bit of powdered cloves to my rubs and sauces. I don't want you to be able to taste the cloves. However, that little bit will give you a hint of the earthiness that you get from chilies. (Elanor does talk about this recipe in the book.)

**Ingredients:**

1/4 c dark cocoa powder

1/4 c instant coffee (I use an instant Italian esspresso)

1/4 c finely ground black pepper

2 T brown sugar

1 T cinnamon

1 t nutmeg

1 t ginger

**Instructions:**

Mix together. Apply liberaly to pork or beef. Makes a good bark on brisket.


## NO NIGHTSHADES BBQ SAUCE

**Ingredients:**

3 C chopped rhubarb

1/4 C water

3 T molasses

3 T maple syrup

2 T apple cider vinegar

1 T garlic powder

1/2 t ground ginger

1 t smoked sea salt OR 1 t Lapsang Souchang tea, finely ground

**Instructions:**

Combine all of the ingredients in a medium sized sauce pan and bring to a low-boil on medium heat.

Turn down the heat and allow to simmer for 25-30 minutes, until the sauce is reduced by half and the rhubarb is very soft.

Transfer mixture to a blender and blend until smooth, then pour the sauce into a mason jar for later use, and store in the fridge. (Be careful if you use an immersion blender! The sauce is hot and I usually end up splashing it everywhere.)

# Read More!

Do you enjoy exploring strange new worlds, new cultures, new people?

Journey into the various lands envisioned by Leah R Cutter.

## READ MORE!

Sign up for my newsletter and I'll start you on your travels with a free copy of my book, *The Island Sampler*.

http://www.LeahCutter.com/newsletter/

# About the Author

Leah R Cutter tells page-turning, wildly creative stories that always leave you guessing in the middle, but completely satisfied by the end.

She writes mystery of all sorts. Her Water Witch paranormal mysteries have well received by readers, who describe it as a lovely weekend read with a cup of tea by the window. Lake Hope cozy mysteries are also well loved.

Her Halley Brown series, revolving around a private investigator who used to be with the Seattle Police Department, leaves you guessing at every turn. And her speculative mysteries, such as the Alvin Goodfellow Case Files—a 1930s PI set on the moon—have garnered great reviews.

She's been published in magazines such as *Alfred Hitchcock's Mystery Magazine* and in anthologies like *Fiction River: Spies*. On top of that, Leah is the editor of the quarterly mystery magazine: *Mystery, Crime, and Mayhem*.

Read more books by Leah Cutter at www.KnottedRoad-Press.com.

Follow her blog at www.LeahCutter.com.

Read more mysteries at www.MCM-Magazine.com

### Reviews

It's true. Reviews help me sell more books. If you've

enjoyed this story, please consider leaving a review of it on your favorite site.

**Come someplace new...**
Do you enjoy exploring strange new worlds, new cultures, new people?

Journey into the various lands envisioned by Leah R Cutter.

Sign up for my newsletter and I'll start you on your travels with a free copy of my book, *The Island Sampler.*

http://www.LeahCutter.com/newsletter/

**Buy More!**
Did you know that you can buy directly from the Knotted Road Press website?

https://www.knottedroadpress.com/shop/

# About Knotted Road Press

Knotted Road Press publishes dynamic fiction set in exotic locations. Our authors cover a wide range of genres including science fiction, fantasy, mystery, literary, and poetry. We also have unique non-fiction voices in genres such as autobiography, business, cookbooks, and how-tos. We offer both DRM-free ebooks and print books for a global readership.

Knotted Road Press
www.KnottedRoadPress.com